Little Orphan Annie

By

HAROLD GRAY■

Edited and with an Introduction by Rick Marschall

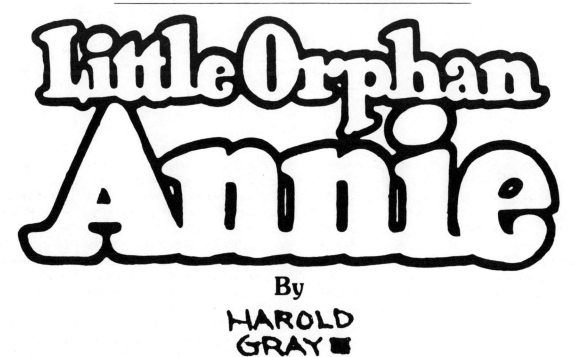

WHAT A YOUNGSTER!
JUST A KID; YET, IN
SOME WAYS, SHE'S A
THOUSAND YEARS OLD—
HAVING TO SHIFT FOR
HERSELF HAS MADE
HER WISE BEYOND HER
YEARS, YET IT HASN'T
SOURED OR SPOILED HER—
SHE HAS THE RIGHT
STUFF IN HER—

FANTAGRAPHICS BOOKS

FANTAGRAPHICS BOOKS
1800 Bridgegate Street #101
Westlake Village, CA 91361

Art direction by Audu Paden.
Series designed by Dale Crain.
Production assistance by Maria Savage and Mark Thompson.
Typesetting by Kim Thompson.

Fantagraphics would like to acknowledge the kind assistance of the Special
Collections, Mugar Memorial Library, Boston University, Howart Gotlieb,
director, and Margaret Goostray, assistant director.

First Fantagraphics Books edition: April, 1988.
10 9 8 7 6 5 4 3 2 1

ISBN: 0-930193-60-1

Library of Congress Catalog Number: 84-81462

Printed in the U.S.A.

Exceptions Proving Rules

By Rick Marschall

Harold Gray's was one of the most cohesive and organic worlds created in the comics. As a comic-strip Expressionist, his artwork perfectly mirrored the literary themes and obsessions of his text. Characters were consistent. Readers knew that bad guys were always bad—and as bad as bad could be—and that justice followed transgression as surely as day followed night.

In *Little Orphan Annie,* these were not creative ruts, just the narrative and structural *givens* of Harold Gray's world. He issued the passwords to enter those worlds visited by Annie through the years, and the *a priori* travel codes, as it were, all were on his terms, not any reader's own set of standards or expectations. I once knew a crusty newspaperwoman whose independence rankled a new editor assigned to our paper. "You do just whatever you damn well please, don't you?" he challenged, exasperated, one day. "That's right," she calmly replied, not looking up from her copy; "and now that we understand that, we can get on with things." So it was for the reader of *Little Orphan Annie:* Gray's ontology was fiercely personal, and you had to take it on his terms. Most readers in America did.

To varying degrees, all strips operate

GRAB HER! SHE MUSTN'T GET AWAY—.I'M TAKING HER TO THE REFORMATORY—

S.S.S.

Reg. U. S. Pat. Off.: Copyright, 1932, by The Chicago Trib

thusly, but Harold Gray's structures and settings, characterizations and sympathies, were so compelling as to make ground rules an issue at all. Other strips permeated by their cartoonists' personal voice had defenders and detractors as did *Annie.* But oftentimes those who disliked the strips simply avoided them; *Joe Palooka, Pogo,* and

Doonesbury come to mind. Somehow that was never the case with Harold Gray's *Little Orphan Annie,* and the reason seems to be that his world was fictional but ultra-realistic at the same time—every element of the strip was an emblem not just attracting attention but demanding reactions. The foremost vehicle for Gray's subterranean messages was his consistency.

But it was not always so; not 100 percent of the time.

The reason we have chosen 1931 as the year to begin this series of reprint books (in Volume 1) is because that is the year that Gray dropped the vestigial pretenses of *Little Orphan Annie* being a kid's strip; Sunday pages previously dabbled in (or weakly attempted) humor. Also, it was the year that Sundays and daily strips began to integrate themselves (it becomes irrevocable practice with the pages in this volume). By the way, eventually *The NEMO Bookshelf Series* will reprint the early years of Annie too, from her "birth" in 1924.

In this volume, reprinting the entire year of 1932, we find what is probably the last fine-tuning Harold Gray ever did with his characters' personalities and the premises of his strip.

Long-time readers will perhaps be surprised to see "Daddy" Warbucks not only take a wife but be mercilessly henpecked for weeks on end. As for the marriage, many fans know that when the strip began he was married, and henpecked too, but that in those seminal episodes Oliver Warbucks was meant to portray a semi-realistic Jiggs (of *Bringing Up Father*); not only did his circumstances befit the dilemma for Annie in that particular story, but he was likely meant never to appear again.

But incidental characters have a way of lingering; "Daddy" was one, and Popeye was to be another. However, once the character of Warbucks was established, it seems strange to see him take a wife—after all, he stands as the prototypical Loner, Strong Man, a Solitary Force—and be almost instantaneously transformed into a wimp.

It was fully consistent with Harold Gray's treatment of the Warbucks character (in terms of "Daddy's" personality and narrative construction both) to have him lose his fortune, his sight, his self-respect even, and, in what was more of a *motif* than a literary reprise, his life or close to it. But not his manhood.

Yet it seems Gray was attempting to chip away at the persona and reveal a humanizing facet. Many might argue that it didn't ring true, and chief amongst them was likely Gray himself, who virtually abandoned experimentation with such an aspect of the Warbucks figure. Henceforth "Daddy" rapidly assumed less human, and more mythic traits.

We see in the strips following another personality-revelation that Gray seldom utilized afterwards, and that is Annie's socialization with contemporaries. After the sequences collected in this book, Gray only occasionally even *depicted* Annie at school, playing with, or speaking to, children her own age. When it did happen, it was either under duress (placed in a home, forced to attend classes), as an alien (rejected as too honest or industrious), or as a lightning agent of charity; and her gifts were as often spiritual as material—as in a 1936 episode where she delivers sustenance to a Depression-ravaged family but offers a palpably more beneficial sermon with Theodore Roosevelt as a role model for the near-sighted boy she visits.

Such visits were invariably awkward for Annie—although not usually between 1924 and 1932, when more frequently her companions, or at least her audiences, were children. It is to be presumed that as her strip-companions grew in median age, so too did her average reader. Annie became no less a mythic figure than Warbucks after 1932, but her role was different.

Her role was not only different than Warbucks's, but radically different from that which was originally assigned her by Gray and the publisher Captain Patterson. In the beginning she was vulnerable on three counts: she was a girl, she was young, and she was an orphan. By 1932 these traits were not only softening, but they were becoming irrelevant.

The remarkable aspect of Annie's personality was to be her invulnerability, not her vulnerability. She was indeed alien to the environments in which Harold Gray set her; and if she seemed fresh and startling to such adults as farmers, shopkeepers, and international smugglers, then her appearance amongst children—even though, by the eye, they *seemed* to be of her age and demeanor—was unnatural.

Exceptions prove rules, however; and even an artist employing such cohesion and organic development as did Harold Gray still, after all, has to develop. Besides some notable adventures, we see in this book some of that interesting developmental process of Harold Gray.

The Window Shopper

A String of Beads

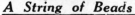

What's the Game?

2

Warbucks Investigates

Wun Wey

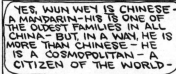

Annie Makes a Friend

4

The Master Is Out

O, About Last Night

Curiosity

A. W. O. L. Again

"DADDY" WAS OUT MONDAY EVENING, AND HE'S GONE OUT AGAIN TO-NIGHT - AND HE NEVER TOLD ME HE WAS GOIN' OUT EITHER TIME - WELL, IT'S AFTER TEN AND I'M NOT GOIN' TO SIT UP FOR HIM ANY LONGER -

WHAT TH' SAM HILL CAN BE KEEPIN' HIM OUT LIKE THAT? COURSE I'M CURIOUS - WHO WOULDN'T BE? IT'S NOT LIKE "DADDY" AT ALL -

WELL, IF HE DOESN'T WANT TO S'PLAIN IT TO ME, HE DOESN'T HAVE TO - WHADDAH I CARE? I'M GOIN' TO GO TO SLEEP AND FORGET 'BOUT IT - HE CAN STAY OUT ALL NIGHT, IF HE WANTS TO -

SH-H-H - YEP - THERE HE COMES IN NOW - I CAN HEAR HIM TIP-TOEIN' TO HIS ROOM - WELL, HE GOT HOME SAFE, ANYWAY, EVEN IF IT DID TAKE HIM TILL ONE-THIRTY -

HAROLD GRAY

Reg. U. S. Pat. Off., Copyright, 1932, by The Chicago Tribune

Squaring Himself

YES - YES - GOOD-BYE - I'LL CALL YOU BACK LATER -

OH, HELLO, "DADDY" - I'VE BEEN LOOKING ALL OVER FOR YOU - I DIDN'T KNOW WHERE YOU WERE -

OH; HA' HA! YES, I WAS TELEPHONING - THAT IS, I GUESS SOME ONE HAD THE WRONG NUMBER -

ARE YOU GOING OUT AGAIN THIS EVENING, "DADDY"?

GOING OUT? WHO, ME? I SHOULD SAY NOT!

BUT TOMORROW EVENING WE'RE BOTH GOING OUT - DINNER AND AFTER THAT I HAVE TICKETS FOR A SHOW I THINK YOU'LL LIKE - HOW DOES THAT STRIKE YOU?

OH, "DADDY"

HAROLD GRAY

Reg. U. S. Pat. Off.; Copyright, 1932, by The Chicago Tribune

A Big Night

WHAT A KICK SHE'S GETTING OUT OF THIS - AND WHAT A BUM "DADDY" I'VE BEEN TO HER LATELY, NEGLECTING HER THE WAY I HAVE - I HAVEN'T MEANT TO NEGLECT HER - EVERYTHING I DO IS FOR HER HAPPINESS -

GEE, THAT WAS A SWELL RESTAURANT WE ATE AT TO-NIGHT - MUSIC AN' FLOWERS - AND SUCH FOOD - AND THAT WAS TH' FUNNIEST SHOW I EVER SAW - WHEN THAT GUY WITH TH' FUNNY PANTS FELL ALL TH' WAY DOWN STAIRS I THOUGHT I'D DIE LAUGHIN' - WASN'T HE A KNOCKOUT?

GOOD-NIGHT, ANNIE - SLEEP TIGHT AND PLEASANT DREAMS -

GOOD-NIGHT, "DADDY" - I'LL BET I DREAM 'BOUT THAT SHOW ALL NIGHT -

IT'S A FUNNY WORLD, SANDY - SOME TIMES I HARDLY KNOW WHAT TO DO - HOW CAN AN OLD DUFFER LIKE I AM, HOPE TO BRING UP A LITTLE TYKE LIKE THAT SO SHE'LL ALWAYS BE HAPPY - I HAVE A PLAN - IF IT ONLY WORKS OUT AS I HOPE - BUT, SO FAR, IT'S A SECRET, SANDY -

Reg. U. S. Pat. Off.; Copyright, 1932, by The Chicago Tribune

Out Again

Too Fast for Annie

Bill Is Worried

The Little Student

Trixie Tinkle

What Was the Name?

Ah Ha!

I DON'T BLAME ANNIE FOR BEING SORT OF UPSET— IT IS A MYSTERY WHERE WARBUCKS HAS BEEN SPENDING SO MUCH OF HIS TIME LATELY— OH-OH!!! WHAT'S THIS?

SO THAT'S IT— JUST AS WELL THEY DIDN'T SEE ME— IF OLIVER HAD WANTED ME TO KNOW, HE'D HAVE TOLD ME— HMM·M·M·—

WELL, I MIGHT HAVE GUESSED IT— WONDER WHO THE LADY IS— I'VE SEEN THAT DAME SOME PLACE—

Bill Takes Sandy's Advice

CHEE— SEEIN' OLIVER WITH A DAME LAST EVENING SURE HANDED ME A SURPRISE— I HOPE HE DOESN'T GO AND MAKE A SAP OF HIMSELF—

STILL, THERE'S NOTHING ANYBODY CAN DO ABOUT IT, I GUESS— HE'S OLD ENOUGH TO KNOW HIS OWN BUSINESS— ON THE OTHER HAND, THERE'S NO FOOL LIKE AN OLD FOOL, THEY SAY—

YOU'RE NO FOOL, SANDY— WHAT DO YOU THINK ABOUT IT? SUPPOSE WARBUCKS SHOULD FALL FOR SOME SMART DAME, HOW WOULD IT AFFECT YOU AND ANNIE, EH? WHAT WOULD YOU DO?

HM·M·M·· NOT A WORD, EH? GUESS YOU'RE RIGHT AT THAT, SANDY— WE'LL JUST KEEP OUR EYES OPEN AND OUR LIPS BUTTONED AND SEE WHAT HAPPENS—

Deficient "Daddy"

GEE, "DADDY"— IT'S AWFUL LONESOME WHEN YOU AREN'T HOME— YOU NEVER USED TO GO OUT SO MUCH, TILL JUST LATELY—

WHY, I GUESS YOU'RE RIGHT, ANNIE— I'LL ARRANGE TO BE HOME MORE REGULARLY VERY SOON NOW—

OH, IF YOU ONLY WOULD, "DADDY"— I MISS YOU SO, WHEN YOU'RE GONE—

DON'T YOU WORRY, ANNIE— IT WON'T BE LONG TILL I'LL BE HOME MOST OF THE TIME—

POOR LITTLE TYKE— OF COURSE, SHE'S LONESOME— WHAT DOES AN OLD WAR HORSE, LIKE I AM, KNOW ABOUT MAKING A REAL HOME FOR A SWEET LITTLE YOUNGSTER LIKE ANNIE—

INCOMPETENT— THAT'S WHAT I AM— I MEAN WELL, BUT, AFTER ALL, I'M JUST AN OLD FUMBLER— I'VE KNOWN IT FOR A LONG WHILE— WHAT ANNIE NEEDS IS THE LOVE AND CARE OF A REAL MOTHER—

11

Satisfied

IS "DADDY" HOME?

'E JUST CAME IN, MISS ANNIE- YOU'LL FIND 'IM IN THE DRAWING ROOM-

HELLO, "DADDY"- GEE, I'M GLAD YOU'RE HOME-

HELLO, ANNIE - COME AROUND HERE- I WANT TO TALK TO YOU - YOUR OLD "DADDY'S" BEEN DOING SOME MIGHTY HEAVY THINKING HERE LATELY -

I REALIZE I HAVEN'T BEEN A VERY GOOD "DADDY" TO YOU SOME TIMES, ANNIE- BUT I DON'T KNOW HOW I COULD HAVE ACTED DIFFERENTLY- I'VE DONE THE BEST I KNOW TO RAISE YOU AND GIVE YOU A GOOD HOME- BUT A FINE HOUSE DOESN'T MAKE A HOME -

WHAT YOU NEED ANNIE, IS A MOTHER- SHE'D LOVE YOU AND UNDERSTAND YOU- WOULDN'T YOU LIKE A REAL MAMA, ANNIE?

AW, GEE - YOU'VE ALWAYS BEEN SWELL TO ME, "DADDY"- IF YOU JUST DON'T GO AWAY AND LEAVE ME ALONE AGAIN, I'LL BE SATISFIED ALWAYS!

Cause for Alarm

LEAPIN' LIZARDS! WHAT "DADDY" SAID YESTERDAY JUST SOAKED IN- I MEAN THAT CRACK 'BOUT ME NEEDIN' A REAL MAMA TO LOOK OUT FOR ME- I DIDN'T THINK ANYTHING ABOUT IT AT THE TIME-

BUT, GEE WHIZ! I WONDER IF HE MEANT THAT- YOU DON'T S'POSE "DADDY'S" FIGGERIN' ON GETTIN' MARRIED, DO YOU, SANDY?

AND IF HE IS, HE MUST HAVE SOMEBODY PICKED OUT- WHO CAN SHE BE? NO TELLIN' HOW A THING LIKE THAT WOULD TURN OUT-

STILL, "DADDY'S" AWFUL SMART- IT MIGHT BE O.K.- MAYBE THERE'S NOTHIN' TO IT, ANYWAY- STILL, HE NEVER TALKED LIKE THAT BEFORE- I'M GOING TO ASK BILL- HE MIGHT KNOW SOMETHIN'-

Who's the Blond?

BUT "DADDY'S" BEEN ACTIN' SORTA FUNNY LATELY - AND HE ASKED ME HOW I'D LIKE A REAL MAMA- HAS HE SAID ANYTHING TO YOU ABOUT IT, BILL?

NOT A WORD, ANNIE-

GEE - I'D SURE HATE TO HAVE "DADDY" GO AN' GET MARRIED, JUST ON MY ACCOUNT-

FORGET IT, ANNIE - YOUR "DADDY" IS A MIGHTY SMART GUY, AND DON'T YOU EVER FORGET IT- HE WAS JUST KIDDIN' YOU, I GUESS-

SO HE'S BEEN ASKING ANNIE HOW SHE'D LIKE A MAMA, EH? THAT'S SUSPICIOUS- SOUNDS LIKE HE MIGHT BE SERIOUS- OF COURSE I COULDN'T LET ON BEFORE ANNIE, BUT I'LL ADMIT THIS HAS ME WORRIED-

NOW THAT DAME I SAW HIM WITH THE OTHER EVENING- WHO IS SHE, ANYWAY? AND WHERE DID WARBUCKS MEET HER? I'VE SEEN THAT BIG BLONDE SOME PLACE- BUT WHERE AND WHEN? HM-M-M-

HAROLD GRAY

12

Bill Remembers

GOING OUT, EH?

YES, BILL — HAVE TO KEEP AN APPOINTMENT — TELL ANNIE NOT TO SIT UP FOR ME — I MAY NOT BE ABLE TO GET HOME TILL QUITE LATE —

AN APPOINTMENT, EH? YEAH — A DATE FOR THE SHOW AND SUPPER WITH THAT BIG BLOND I SAW HIM WITH — HE CAN'T FOOL ME — FUNNY I CAN'T PLACE THAT DAME — I'VE SEEN HER AND I KNOW HER — BUT I JUST CAN'T SEEM TO REMEMBER — — — —

NOW I REMEMBER!!! SURE — WHY, THAT'S TRIXIE TINKLE — SHE WAS A HEADLINER ON BROADWAY FIFTEEN OR TWENTY YEARS AGO — LET'S SEE — HER REAL NAME WAS BLOB — ELIZA BLOB — YES SIR — TRIXIE TINKLE —

WELL, SHE WAS ALWAYS A NICE GIRL — NEVER GOT MIXED UP IN ANY NEWS-PAPER SCANDALS OR ANYTHING — ALWAYS A PERFECT LADY, AS I REMEMBER IT — I SUPPOSE WARBUCKS COULD DO WORSE — STILL, THE IDEA OF OLIVER FALLING FOR A BIG, FAT BLOND LIKE THAT —

Warbucks' Problem

LIFE SURE IS FUNNY — YOU CAN SCHEME AND PLAN AND HOPE, BUT YOU NEVER CAN SEE ONE INCH INTO THE FUTURE — EVEN TO-MORROW IS ALWAYS A MYSTERY —

NO CHANCE TO SNEAK A LOOK AT THE LAST CHAPTER TO SEE HOW YOUR LIFE IS GOING TO TURN OUT IN THE END — YOU HAVE TO TAKE EACH PAGE AS IT COMES — LIFE'S SORT OF A SERIAL — ONE INSTALLMENT EACH DAY — MAYBE THAT'S WHY LIFE'S SO INTERESTING —

DO YOU KNOW, BILL, I HARDLY KNOW WHAT TO DO ABOUT ANNIE — I CAN'T GIVE HER WHAT A MOTHER COULD — SHE NEEDS THE LOVE AND CARE AND KINDLY INFLUENCE OF A GOOD WOMAN — DON'T YOU AGREE WITH ME?

WELL, YES AND NO — OF COURSE THERE'S NOTHING FINER THAN A REAL MOTHER — STILL, ANNIE SEEMS TO HAVE COME ALONG PRETTY WELL WITHOUT ONE FOR A LONG TIME — I SUPPOSE SHE'D BE BETTER OFF FOR THE INFLUENCE OF THE RIGHT WOMAN — BUT IT WOULD HAVE TO BE ONE WOMAN IN A MILLION TO BE GOOD ENOUGH TO BE ANNIE'S MOTHER — THAT'S WHAT I THINK OF THE KID —

Oriental Tact

HELLO, WUN WEY — I DROPPED IN TO GET SOME OF YOUR ADVICE —

ADVICE IS WORTH JUST WHAT IT COSTS AND MINE COSTS YOU NOTHING — HOWEVER I WILL GIVE IT TO YOU MOST GLADLY —

IT'S ABOUT LITTLE ANNIE — I THINK SHE OUGHT TO HAVE A REAL MOTHER — SOME ONE WHO WOULD LOVE HER AND FOR WHOM SHE WOULD CARE A GREAT DEAL —

I SEE — YES — THE IDEA IS MOST SOUND — A MOTHER IS VERY DESIRABLE —

BUT LIKE SO MANY SOUND IDEAS, THE PRACTICAL APPLICATION PRESENTS MANY PROBLEMS — AS AMERICANS SAY, BLOOD IS THICKER THAN WATER — IT WOULD BE A RARE WOMAN WHO COULD LOVE ANNIE AS DEEPLY AS IF ANNIE WERE HER OWN CHILD —

IT IS EVIDENT OLIVER HAS SOME LADY IN MIND AND HE WISHES TO BE ASSURED THAT THIS LADY WILL BE KIND TO ANNIE — WHEN A MAN HAS HIS MIND MADE UP ABOUT A WOMAN, NO ONE BUT A FOOL WILL TRY TO INTERFERE —

Two Right Guys

History

A Heart as Big as a Whale

The Invitation

HELLO, WUN WEY— I JUST CALLED UP TO SEE IF YOU'D HAD ANY IDEA YET ON HOW WE CAN BREAK UP THIS TRIXIE TINKLE AFFAIR— YEAH— I GUESS YOU'RE RIGHT— WE'LL HAVE TO WATCH FOR AN OPENING— OH, I GUESS THERE'S NO HURRY— WARBUCKS WON'T DO ANYTHING FOOLISH FOR A WHILE— WE HAVE PLENTY OF TIME—

YES, WE MUST WAIT FOR AN OPENING— BUT I DO NOT AGREE THAT WE HAVE PLENTY OF TIME— MY OBSERVATION HAS BEEN THAT WARBUCKS IS A MAN OF QUICK DECISIONS AND SUDDEN ACTION— ONCE HIS MIND IS MADE UP, HE WILL ACT— OUR ONLY CHANCE LIES IN DISSUADING HIM BEFORE HIS MIND IS MADE UP, IF POSSIBLE—

I WISH I COULD BE SURE— IF I ONLY KNEW THAT ANNIE AND TRIXIE WOULD LOVE EACH OTHER— WELL I'LL NEVER BE ABLE TO JUDGE WISELY TILL I'VE SEEN THEM TOGETHER— I'LL CALL UP TRIXIE RIGHT NOW—

DINNER AT YOUR HOME TO-MORROW EVENING? OH, THAT WILL BE LOVELY— AND I'LL MEET YOUR FRIENDS, BILL AND WUN WEY AND DEAR LITTLE ANNIE— OH, I CAN HARDLY— WAIT—

Surprise

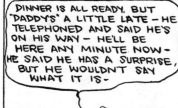

DINNER IS ALL READY, BUT "DADDY'S" A LITTLE LATE— HE TELEPHONED AND SAID HE'S ON HIS WAY— HE'LL BE HERE ANY MINUTE NOW— HE SAID HE HAS A SURPRISE, BUT HE WOULDN'T SAY WHAT IT IS—

HELLO, EVERYBODY— I BROUGHT A LITTLE SURPRISE FOR YOU— MISS TINKLE, THESE ARE MY VERY DEAR FRIENDS I'VE TOLD YOU ABOUT— BILL AND WUN WEY— AND THIS IS LITTLE ANNIE—

HOW DO YOU DO, MISS TINKLE—

HOW DO YOU DO, MISS TINKLE—

OH, OLIVER HAS TOLD ME SUCH WONDERFUL THINGS ABOUT YOU BOTH— I'M SO GLAD TO MEET YOU—

AND THIS IS ANNIE! OH, YOU LITTLE DARLING— SUCH BIG, ROUND EYES! AND WHAT LOVELY, CURLY HAIR— I JUST KNOW WE'RE GOING TO BE GREAT PALS—

A Woman's Spell

WELL, BILL, I GUESS I GAVE YOU A SURPRISE LAST NIGHT WHEN I BROUGHT TRIXIE TINKLE HOME FOR DINNER— WHAT DO YOU THINK OF HER? WONDERFUL GIRL, EH?

YES— YOU SURE DID SURPRISE ME— WHY, SHE SEEMS O.K.— SHE'S AN EX-SHOW GIRL, ISN'T SHE?

HUH— OLIVER MUST HAVE GONE JITTERY TO FALL FOR THAT BIG BLOND— AND THE WAY SHE COOED AND FUSSED OVER ANNIE WOULD GIVE YOU A PAIN IN TH' NECK— CAN'T OLIVER SEE THROUGH THAT GAME? SHE'S JUST USING THAT LINE TO MAKE A HIT WITH HIM, OR I MISS MY GUESS—

MY, THE WAY TRIXIE TOOK TO LITTLE ANNIE— SHE CAN'T FOOL ME— THAT WASN'T PUT ON— THAT WAS REAL— AND ANNIE SEEMED TO LIKE HER, TOO— ANNIE DOESN'T TAKE TO EVERYONE EITHER— IF SHE DOESN'T LIKE SOMEBODY, SHE'S HONEST AND SHOWS IT— BUT SHE LIKES TRIXIE—

OF COURSE I'VE ASKED MYSELF IF SHE'S JUST AFTER SOME OF MY MONEY— I'M AS HARD-BOILED AND CYNICAL AS THE NEXT ONE— BUT SHUX! ONE LOOK AT THOSE HONEST EYES IS ENOUGH— SHOW GIRL OR NO SHOW GIRL— TRIXIE'D MAKE A WONDERFUL MOTHER FOR ANNIE—

As Annie Sees Her

GEE, SANDY - I DON'T KNOW WHAT TO THINK' O' THAT TRIXIE TINKLE - SHE SEEMED NICE - COURSE SHE'S BEEN AN ACTRESS AND WHAT I'M WONDERIN' IS, IS SHE LIKE SHE SEEMS, OR IS SHE STILL ACTIN'?

2-11

"DADDY" THINKS SHE'S WONDERFUL - I WOULDN'T WANT TO KNOCK TRIXIE TO HIM - I WOULDN'T HURT HIS FEELINGS FOR THE WORLD - AND TRIXIE SEEMS CRAZY 'BOUT "DADDY", TOO -

COURSE ANYBODY'D HAVE TO LIKE "DADDY" - HE'S SO DOG-GONED GENEROUS AND SWELL EVERY WAY - BUT I'D HATE LIKE EVER'THING TO SEE HIM MAKE ANY MISTAKE HE'D BE SORRY FOR -

TRIXIE MIGHT BE O.K. - COURSE SHE'S SORTA LOUD AND SHE WEARS AWFUL FLASHY JEWELRY - BUT SHE SEEMS GOOD-NATURED - YOU'VE GOTTA KNOW ANYBODY FOR A WHILE 'FORE YOU CAN REALLY TELL MUCH ABOUT 'EM FOR SURE -

HAROLD GRAY

Reg. U.S. Pat. Off., Copyright, 1932, by The Chicago Tribune

Shopping

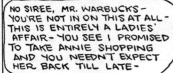

NO SIREE, MR. WARBUCKS - YOU'RE NOT IN ON THIS AT ALL - THIS IS ENTIRELY A LADIES' AFFAIR - YOU SEE I PROMISED TO TAKE ANNIE SHOPPING AND YOU NEEDN'T EXPECT HER BACK TILL LATE -

2-12

YES, THAT LOOKS ALL RIGHT FOR ONE - LET'S SEE ALL YOU HAVE - ANNIE WANTS AT LEAST A DOZEN NEW DRESSES

GEE - THAT'S PRETTY -

ZIS IS ZE LATEST FASHION - AND EET WILL BE SO BECOMING -

OH, THAT IS A PRETTY NECKLACE - BUT IT'S LOTS TOO SWELL FOR ME, TRIXIE -

TOO SWELL FOR YOU! HA-HA-HA! THAT'S A FUNNY ONE - NOTHING IS TOO SWELL, WITH A "DADDY" AS RICH AS YOUR'S, ANNIE -

AND WE HAVE THE BRACELET TO MATCH -

SAY, I DUNNO WHEN I'VE HAD SUCH A SWELL DAY - IT SURE IS FUN TO BUY PRETTY THINGS, ISN'T IT?

YOU SAID IT, ANNIE - AND, WITH YOUR "DADDY'S" MONEY, YOU NEVER HAVE TO WORRY ABOUT PRICES - THE BEST OF IT IS, HE WANTS YOU TO HAVE NICE THINGS - HE'S CERTAINLY A WONDERFUL MAN -

HAROLD GRAY

Reg. U.S. Pat. Off., Copyright, 1932, by The Chicago Tribune

Cause for Alarm

GEE, BILL - YOU SHOULD SEE THE SWELL NEW DRESSES AN' OTHER THINGS TRIXIE HELPED ME BUY YESTERDAY - SHE SURE KNOWS HOW TO SHOP - I HAD A PEACH OF A TIME -

HM-M-M - I DARE SAY - SO TRIXIE WAS PRETTY NICE TO YOU, EH? YOU SORT OF LIKE HER, DON'T YOU?

2-13

HEY! TAXI!!!

LISTEN, WUN WEY - LET'S GO INTO YOUR BACK ROOM WHERE WE CAN TALK - I'VE GOT NEWS - SAY, IS THAT TRIXIE DAME ONE FAST WORKER! AND IS SHE SMOOTH, TOO!

HAROLD GRAY

, 1932, by The Chicago Tribune

SHE TOOK ANNIE SHOPPING YESTERDAY - HELPED HER GET A LOT OF SWELL STUFF - OF COURSE THE KID IS TICKLED AND THINKS TRIXIE IS WONDERFUL - GET IT? GETTIN' TH' KID ON HER SIDE ALREADY -

YES, A VERY SOUND BIT OF STRATEGY ON HER PART - SHE IS A CLEVER WOMAN - IF WE ARE TO STOP THIS, WE MUST ACT QUICKLY -

19

Two Viewpoints

IF IT WERE NOT FOR ANNIE I DON'T THINK I'D EVEN CONSIDER GETTING MARRIED AGAIN— NOT THAT TRIXIE ISN'T WONDERFUL— BUT IT'S HER APPARENT LOVE FOR CHILDREN, AND ESPECIALLY FOR ANNIE, THAT IMPRESSES ME—

TRIXIE MAY BE EXTRAVAGANT— MY MONEY MAY IMPRESS HER UNDULY— WHAT OF IT? WHAT DO I CARE HOW MUCH SHE SPENDS, IF SHE MAKES ANNIE HAPPY? MAYBE I'M AN OLD FOOL, BUT I WANT ANNIE TO BE HAPPY—

TRIXIE MAY TURN OUT ALL RIGHT— IT'S HARD TO TELL— SHE'S SURE BEEN SWELL TO ME SO FAR— SHE TOOK ME SHOPPING AND TO A SHOW AND BOUGHT ME CANDY AND ICE CREAM— COURSE SHE'S SORTA LOUD AN' FLASHY, BUT, IF SHE'S NICE TO "DADDY", THAT'S THE MAIN THING—

IF SHE SHOULD MARRY "DADDY" SHE MIGHT NOT ALWAYS BE SO NICE TO ME— STILL, "DADDY'S" SURE GONE THROUGH A HEAP FOR ME— GUESS I COULD PUT UP WITH A LITTLE FOR HIM— ANYWAY, THEY'RE NOT MARRIED YET—

2-15 Reg. U.S. Pat. Off.; Copyright, 1932, by The Chicago Tribune.

The Friends' Meeting

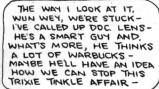

THE WAY I LOOK AT IT, WUN WEY, WE'RE STUCK— I'VE CALLED UP DOC. LENS— HE'S A SMART GUY AND, WHAT'S MORE, HE THINKS A LOT OF WARBUCKS— MAYBE HE'LL HAVE AN IDEA HOW WE CAN STOP THIS TRIXIE TINKLE AFFAIR—

HELLO, DOC.— COME IN— WE'RE WAITING FOR YOU—

WE AWAIT YOUR WORDS OF WISDOM, DOCTOR—

I'M AFRAID I WON'T BE ABLE TO HELP MUCH—

IT'S NEXT TO IMPOSSIBLE TO STOP A MAN FROM MARRYING HIS CHOICE, ESPECIALLY A MAN WITH WARBUCKS' DETERMINATION— BUT I BELIEVE IN FRANKNESS— MY SUGGESTION IS THAT EACH ONE OF US GO TO HIM AND HAVE A FRANK TALK ON THE SUBJECT— HE MUST BE SWAYED, TO SOME EXTENT, BY THE VIEWS OF HIS CLOSEST FRIENDS—

THAT'S A GOOD HUNCH, DOC— I'LL HAVE IT OUT WITH HIM TO-MORROW—

MIND YOU, I DON'T GUARANTEE THAT IT WILL DO MUCH GOOD IN THE LONG-RUN—

ONE CAN ONLY TRY—

2-16 Reg. U.S. Pat. Off.; Copyright, 1932 by The Chicago Tribune.

Strong Sales Resistance

I TELL YOU, OLIVER, IT'S THE BIGGEST MISTAKE YOU COULD MAKE— THAT DAME IS JUST AFTER YOUR MONEY— THEY'RE ALL ALIKE— DON'T BE A SAP— I REALIZE I MAY QUEER MYSELF WITH YOU FOREVER BY TALKING LIKE THIS— BUT I LIKE YOU WELL ENOUGH TO RISK IT— SEE?

THAT'S ALL RIGHT, BILL— GO AHEAD—

HE WOULDN'T EVEN ARGUE WITH ME— JUST SAT THERE AND LISTENED TO ALL I SAID— GRINNED AND TOLD ME NOT TO WORRY— WHAT CAN YOU DO WITH A GUY LIKE THAT? HE PROBABLY FIGURES I DON'T UNDERSTAND, BECAUSE I'M AN UGLY LITTLE CRIPPLE— I UNDERSTAND, WELL ENOUGH— TOO WELL—

POOR BILL— HE MEANS WELL— SO SHE IS JUST AFTER MY MONEY AND THEY'RE ALL ALIKE, EH? THAT'S WHAT HE THINKS— BUT HE DOESN'T KNOW TRIXIE LIKE I KNOW TRIXIE— STILL, I CAN SEE BILL'S POINT OF VIEW, ALL RIGHT—

THE POOR CHAP— HE'S BEEN A CRIPPLE ALL HIS LIFE— NATURALLY HE'S CYNICAL— I'LL BET I'VE BEEN THE FIRST REAL FRIEND HE'S EVER HAD, AND I'LL REMAIN HIS FRIEND, NO MATTER WHAT HAPPENS— BUT HE FEARS TRIXIE MAY RUIN OUR FRIENDSHIP— HE'S JEALOUS— POOR BILL—

2-17 Reg. U.S. Pat. Off.; Copyright, 1932, by The Chicago Tribune.

HAROLD GRAY

No Sale

Panel 1: I HOPE YOU WILL PARDON THE IMPERTINENCE OF MY REMARKS— I MERELY FELT IMPELLED TO EXPRESS MY VIEWS ON A SUBJECT WHICH, AFTER ALL, IS YOUR PERSONAL AFFAIR—

THAT'S QUITE ALL RIGHT, WUN WEY— BUT I THINK YOU WILL CHANGE YOUR MIND, WHEN YOU KNOW TRIXIE BETTER—

Panel 2: I FEAR MY GEMS OF ADVICE WILL PROVE OF SMALL VALUE TO HIM— HIS MIND IS MADE UP— I FEAR IT IS FUTILE TO ATTEMPT TO DIVERT THE COURSE OF THE AVALANCHE WITH WORDS—

Panel 3: GOOD OLD WUN WEY— TRYING TO SAVE ME— HE'S STILL AN ORIENTAL AT HEART, AFTER ALL— HE HAS THE WRONG SLANT ON THIS THING ENTIRELY— BUT I DON'T BLAME HIM— HE MEANT ALL HE SAID FOR THE BEST—

Panel 4: WHAT DID WUN WEY WANT TO SEE YOU ABOUT, "DADDY"?

OH, NOTHING SPECIAL, ANNIE— UP YOU GO! WHEE! WELL, THANK GOODNESS YOU AND SANDY STILL GIVE YOUR OLD "DADDY" CREDIT FOR KNOWING HOW TO RUN HIS OWN BUSINESS—

2-18

Out of Bounds

Panel 1: YES, DOCTOR— I'LL THINK OVER WHAT YOU SAID— MIGHTY GLAD YOU DROPPED IN—

THANKS, MR. WARBUCKS— AND I HOPE YOU WON'T FEEL I WAS TOO PERSONAL— A DOCTOR'S PREROGATIVE, YOU KNOW—

Panel 2: NO— I'M AFRAID I MADE NO IMPRESSION ON HIM AT ALL— OH, YES— HE WAS PERFECTLY POLITE— TOO POLITE— HE AGREED WITH ALMOST EVERYTHING I SAID— YOU'RE RIGHT, BILL— HE'S A HARD CUSTOMER—

2-19

Panel 3: DOC. LENS, OF ALL PEOPLE— GREAT SCOTT— NO-BODY ASKED <u>HIM</u> TO MARRY TRIXIE— AFTER ALL, <u>I'M</u> THE ONE WHO IS MOST AFFECTED — — AND LITTLE ANNIE —

Panel 4: HE'S LIKE A LOT OF DOCTORS— SMART IN THEIR OWN LINE, BUT SUCKERS OUT OF IT— AND ALWAYS TAMPERING WITH OTHER PEOPLE'S PERSONAL AFFAIRS— OF COURSE HE MEANS WELL— BUT I WISH MY FRIENDS WOULD QUIT TRYING TO HANDLE MY PERSONAL AFFAIRS FOR ME— I'M GETTING SICK OF THEIR MEDDLING—

Doubt

Panel 1: WELL, TRIXIE, I WISH YOU LUCK—

YEAH— WELL, I'M TELLING YOU, GYPSY GAY, I SURE NEED ALL THE LUCK I CAN GET—

2-20

Panel 2: WHAT'S THE MATTER WITH THE OLD GOOF— IF HE'S GOING TO PROPOSE, WHY DOESN'T HE PROPOSE? YOU'VE GIVEN HIM PLENTY OF CHANCES, HAVEN'T YOU?

CHANCES! HUH! THAT MAN IS DIFFERENT FROM ANY BIRD I EVER SAW— HE'S NO SUCKER—

Panel 3: RICH AND SINGLE— A PERFECT SET-UP— BUT ALL THE REGULAR LINES LEAVE HIM COLD— IT'S THAT BRAT, ANNIE— IF I DON'T GO INTO RAPTURES OVER <u>HER</u>, I DON'T GET TO FIRST BASE WITH <u>HIM</u>— WELL, I'VE DONE MY BEST TO BE A PERFECT "MUVVER" TO HER— UGH! EVEN SO, IF THE BRAT DOESN'T GO FOR <u>ME</u> IN A BIG WAY, I'M SUNK—

Panel 4: I THINK THE KID IS FALLING FOR ME, BUT I CAN'T BE SURE— SHE'S SMART— IF I CAN GET HER ON MY SIDE, I'LL BE ON THE SUNNY-SIDE OF EASY-STREET—

IMAGINE! AN ORPHAN BRAT LIKE THAT STANDING BETWEEN YOU AND MILLIONS— WELL, GOOD LUCK, TRIXIE—

22

The Other Side

TELL ME, TRIXIE - DO YOU REALLY LOVE THIS BALD-HEADED OLD GUY, WARBUCKS?

THE IDEA, GYPSY GAY - DO I LOVE HIM? WITH HIS BILLIONS? HE COULD BE AS OLD AS SANTA CLAUS; WITH HIS DOUGH AND I'D STILL BE CRAZY ABOUT HIM -

SERIOUSLY, GYPSY - I THINK I DO LOVE HIM - REALLY HE'S NOT SO BAD - HE'S BEEN EVERYWHERE - HE NEVER BORES ONE BY REPEATING HIMSELF - HE'S SURE NO LOUNGE-LIZARD, EITHER - AND HE'S NOT SO OLD - IT WAS A TERRIBLE TROPICAL FEVER MADE HIS HAIR FALL OUT - I THINK I COULD LIKE HIM A LOT, EVEN WITHOUT HIS MONEY -

HM-M-M - SO SHE THINKS SHE COULD LIKE HIM WITHOUT HIS MONEY, EH? WELL, MAYBE - BUT IT'S A LOT EASIER TO LOVE HIM WITH IT - TRIXIE'S A GOOD SOUL - WE'VE BEEN THROUGH A LOT TOGETHER - OF COURSE SHE'S REGULAR - SHE'S OUT FOR THE BIG MONEY - WHO CAN BLAME HER - SHE'S GOT TO LOOK AHEAD -

THE SHOW GAME IS NO CINCH, EVEN WHEN YOU'RE YOUNG - AND TRIXIE IS GETTING ALONG - SHE'S ON THE LEVEL IN EVERY WAY, TOO - IF SHE LIKES THIS WARBUCKS' PARTY, I HOPE SHE GETS HIM - HE COULD SURE DO LOTS WORSE THAN TO MARRY TRIXIE - SHE'S TOO GOOD FOR ANY MAN -

Old Fashioned "Daddy"

OH, ONCE OUT OF THE SWAMP IT WAS EASY - TWO WEEKS LATER WE REACHED THE MOUTH OF THE RIVER WHERE THE SCHOONER WAS WAITING FOR US -

GEE, "DADDY" - YOU SURE HAVE BEEN IN SOME TIGHT PLACES - AND DID YOU EVER SEE THE OLD NATIVE CHIEF AGAIN?

YES, ANNIE - BUT THAT'S ANOTHER STORY ALL BY ITSELF - DON'T YOU THINK IT'S ABOUT BED TIME FOR LITTLE GIRLS LIKE YOU?

GUESS YOU'RE RIGHT, "DADDY" - I DIDN'T REALIZE IT WAS SO LATE - GOOD-NIGHT, "DADDY" -

"DADDY" SURE WAS HIS REGULAR OLD SELF TO-NIGHT - GEE, I COULD LISTEN FOREVER, WHEN HE TELLS STORIES OF THE PLACES HE'S BEEN AND THE 'VENTURES HE'S HAD - HE'S SURE SEEN THE WORLD -

YESSIR - HE WAS JUST LIKE HE USED TO BE, TO-NIGHT - MAYBE HE'S FORGOTTEN ALL ABOUT THIS TRIXIE TINKLE DAME - MAYBE WE GOT ALL 'CITED 'BOUT HER FOR NOTHING -

Love Is Blind

I HAVE SOME NEWS FOR YOU, WUN WEY - A FRIEND OF YOURS WAS IN MY SHOP YESTERDAY - MR. OLIVER WARBUCKS - I THOUGHT YOU WOULD BE INTERESTED -

YES?

HE BOUGHT OUR FINEST DIAMOND NECKLACE - PAID CASH AND TOOK IT WITH HIM - AS YOU KNOW, IT IS THE FINEST NECKLACE IN THIS COUNTRY - WHAT DO YOU THINK OF THAT? HAS HE FALLEN FOR SOME DAME?

WHO CAN SAY? PERHAPS HE ADMIRES BEAUTIFUL AND COSTLY STONES FOR THEMSELVES ALONE -

MY WORTHY FRIEND, THE JEWELER FROM THE AVENUE, WASTES TIME IN SEEKING INFORMATION HERE - SO OLIVER HAS PURCHASED A COSTLY NECKLACE, UNDOUBTEDLY FOR MISS TRIXIE TINKLE - THAT IS NOT SO GOOD - STILL, IT MAY MEAN NOTHING - IT MAY BE THAT, WITH A GIFT, HE BIDS FARE-WELL TO THE LADY -

OLIVER IS A VERY WISE MAN - CAN HE BE SO STUPID WHERE THIS WOMAN IS CONCERNED - HUH?

LOVE IS BLIND - LOVE IS BLIND -

Pals

On the Side Lines

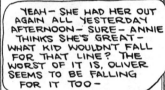

Wun Wey's Hunch

25

Here Comes the Bride

Reactions

The New Mama

Nothing Escapes Annie

Face Value

Buy, Baby Buy-O

Little Orphan Annie

"Daddy" Warbucks has surprised everyone by getting married to Trixie Tinkle - He has felt for a long time that Annie needs a mother's loving care - the idea is sound, but how will it work out?

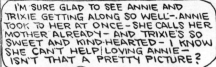

I'm sure glad to see Annie and Trixie getting along so well - Annie took to her at once - she calls her mother already - and Trixie's so sweet and kind-hearted - I know she can't help loving Annie - isn't that a pretty picture?

Gee - it's sure swell to have a real mama I can call my own - Sandy and I are both crazy 'bout you, aren't we, Sandy?

ARF!

Well, no one could help loving a sweet little girl like you - and I'm sure Sandy and I will be great pals - I adore dogs -

She's a wise little brat - too smart to suit me - but one can't expect to grab millions without there being some catch to it -

Oh - it's you, eh? I might have known it -

You big oaf! I may have to be polite to you in front of certain people, but don't get the idea I'd ever go for a mongrel cur like you -

Get out! You and your long hair and FLEAS, like as not - and KEEP away from me - SCRAM!

YIPE!

You won't be around HERE long - I'll see to that - I'm the missus here now and you just don't fit into the picture - SEE?

Oh, hello, mother - I didn't know where you were -

Hello, Annie darling - mother has lost the book she was reading - I wonder if you could try to find it for her -

Sure - I saw it in here a while ago - I'll bring it to you -

Hey - what on earth has happened, Sandy? What's th' matter? Has somebody been mean to you?

HM-M-M---

Reg. U.S. Pat. Off.; Copyright, 1932, by The Chicago Tribune.

28

An Interruption

WELL, WE'RE ALMOST PACKED - THE YACHT IS ALL READY - WE CAN BE OUT OF THE HARBOR AND ON OUR WAY BEFORE DARK - HELLO - WHAT IS IT, HENRY?

HI BEG YOUR PARDON, SIR - YOUR SECRETARY WAS MOST HINSISTENT THAT I TELL YOU - HIT'S SOMETHING TO DO WITH A RADIOGRAM, SIR -

AH - FROM SPIKE MARLIN - WHAT'S THIS? HM-M.. THIS LOOKS SERIOUS - WHY HAVEN'T I BEEN TOLD OF THIS SITUATION BEFORE?

THIS IS THE VERY FIRST INTIMATION OF ANY TROUBLE IN THE ORIENTAL SHIPPING CO - ALL HAS BEEN SERENE TILL THIS RADIO -

YES - YES - WELL, DON'T BOTHER ME WITH THE DIFFICULTIES INVOLVED - I MUST TALK TO SINGAPORE AND SPEAK TO CAPTAIN SPIKE MARLIN PERSONALLY --- AND AT ONCE - I'LL HOLD THE WIRE TILL YOU GET HIM - YES -

WHAT ON EARTH IS UP NOW? AND JUST AS WE ARE ALL READY TO START ON OUR CRUISE -

HOW DO I KNOW WHAT'S UP? THERE'S SOMETHING WRONG WITH MY SHIPPING COMPANY IN THE ORIENT - IT IS IMPORTANT, OR SPIKE MARLIN WOULD NEVER HAVE RADIOED ME ABOUT IT -

3-7

Reg. U. S. Pat. Off. Copyright, 1932, by The Chicago Tribune

HAROLD GRAY

The Trip Is Off

THERE'S NO DOUBT ABOUT IT - I OUGHT TO GO OUT TO SINGAPORE AND STRAIGHTEN THINGS OUT - SPIKE MARLIN MAY BE ABLE TO HANDLE IT ALL RIGHT - HE'S A GOOD MAN - BUT IT'S A BIG JOB FOR ANY ONE MAN -

DO YOU REALIZE WE ARE ALL PACKED UP? THAT WE WERE TO HAVE STARTED ON A LONG CRUISE ON THE YACHT YESTERDAY? WHAT ON EARTH IS THE MATTER? HAVE YOU FORGOTTEN ALL ABOUT IT? IS A LITTLE BUSINESS MORE IMPORTANT THAN OUR HONEYMOON?

YOU DON'T UNDERSTAND, TRIXIE - A LITTLE BUSINESS, AS YOU CALL IT, IN THIS CASE INVOLVES A FLEET OF LINERS AND MODERN FREIGHTERS, THOUSANDS OF MEN AND MORE MILLIONS THAN I WOULD CARE TO LOSE - IN FACT, I CAN'T AFFORD TO LOSE THAT BUSINESS -

IN FACT, IF I FORGET MY BUSINESS AT SUCH A TIME, THERE'S LIABLE TO BE NO YACHT, NO HOME, NO NOTHING - I OUGHT TO GO TO THE ORIENT - HOWEVER I'M GOING TO TRY TO HANDLE IT FROM HERE - BUT I'LL HAVE TO KEEP IN CONSTANT TOUCH WITH SINGAPORE BY 'PHONE - AND UNTIL THERE IS SOME CHANGE, THE YACHT TRIP IS OFF!

3-8

HAROLD GRAY

"Daddy" Explains

SAY, "DADDY" - YOU KNOW HOW CRAZY TO GO ON THAT YACHT TRIP TRIXIE IS - AND YOU SAY YOU OUGHT TO GO TO SINGAPORE? WHY NOT TAKE THE YACHT TRIP AFTER ALL AND ALL OF US GO TO SINGAPORE? TRIXIE'D GET HER BOAT-RIDE AND YOU COULD 'TEND TO YOUR BUSINESS -

COMBINE BUSINESS AND PLEASURE, EH? I THOUGHT OF THAT, BUT IT WON'T WORK - NOW HERE IS WHERE WE ARE AND HERE IS SINGAPORE - EVEN WITH THE YACHT AT FULL SPEED AND WITH PERFECT WEATHER, IT WOULD TAKE OVER A MONTH TO GET THERE - THAT WOULD BE TOO LATE -

GEE - IT IS A LONG WAY - I DIDN'T REALIZE -

NOW, IF I HAD TO GO, I'D GO FAST - PLANES - FLY DAY AND NIGHT - I'D EITHER BE THERE IN FOUR OR FIVE DAYS, OR I'D NEVER GET THERE AT ALL - YOU SEE FLYING ACROSS THE PACIFIC ISN'T SO SURE-FIRE AS IT MIGHT BE - IT'D BE NO TRIP FOR YOU OR TRIXIE - I'D HAVE TO GO ALONE - BUT I'M GOING TO TRY TO HANDLE IT FROM HERE -

ANNIE UNDERSTANDS - BUT POOR TRIXIE - IT'S NO USE TRYING TO EXPLAIN IT TO HER - NEITHER OF THEM CAN REALIZE WHAT IT MIGHT BE LIKE OUT THERE - DANGER - PLENTY OF ROUGH STUFF, MAYBE - PERSONALLY I'D LOVE IT, BUT IT WOULD BE NO PLACE FOR WOMAN -

3-9

Reg. U. S. Pat. Off., Copyright, 1932, by The Chicago Tribune.

HAROLD GRAY

Plans

WELL, THE YACHT TRIP IS OFF, FOR NOW AT LEAST - I CAN'T SEE WHY OLIVER IS SO FUSSED ABOUT SOME BUSINESS MATTER TEN THOUSAND MILES FROM HERE - BUT THERE'S NO USE ARGUING WITH HIM - HM-M-M - THERE'S PLENTY RIGHT HERE TO KEEP ME BUSY -

THIS PLACE IS A MESS - BIG ENOUGH - SWELL VIEW FROM WAY UP HERE FIFTY STORIES ABOVE THE CITY - BUT SUCH TERRIBLE FURNITURE - NO SNAP TO IT - I'LL HAVE TO HAVE THE WHOLE PLACE DONE OVER -

AND THAT BIG LUMMOX! CAN'T YOU JUST SEE HIM BARGING AROUND A SWELL APARTMENT, TRACKING UP THE RUGS, TIPPING OVER THE CHAIRS, SHEDDING HIS LONG HAIR ON ALL THE CUSHIONS - UGH! WHAT A DOG!

I'LL HAVE TO GET RID OF HIM - THAT'S MY FIRST JOB - I'VE GOT TO GO EASY, THOUGH - THE KID IS CRAZY ABOUT HIM - I'LL HAVE TO FIND OUT JUST WHERE I STAND - IMAGINE! ME HAVING TO USE DIPLOMACY IN MY OWN HOME IN DEALING WITH A MONGREL LIKE THAT -

The Uncanny Canine

MY, WHAT A BIG, SHAGGY DOG - IT MUST BE A LOT OF TROUBLE TO KEEP HIM HALF-WAY CLEAN - I'D THINK YOU'D PREFER A SMALLER DOG - ONE WITH SHORT HAIR - THE LITTLE ONES ARE SO MUCH MORE INTELLIGENT, TOO -

OH, I WOULDN'T TRADE SANDY FOR ALL THE OTHER DOGS IN THE WORLD - AND HE'S NEVER DIRTY - HE'S JUST RIGHT - AND SMART? SAY! HE KNOWS OVER A HUNDRED TRICKS - WHY, SANDY AND I HAVE BEEN THROUGH TOO MUCH TO-GETHER - I'LL STICK TO HIM AS LONG AS I LIVE -

OLIVER - DON'T YOU THINK SOMETHING OUGHT TO BE DONE ABOUT SANDY? HE'S SO BIG AND CLUMSY AND OUT OF PLACE IN AN APARTMENT LIKE THIS -

OH, SANDY'S ALL RIGHT - HE'S CAREFUL OF THE FURNITURE AND THERE NEVER WAS A SMARTER WATCH-DOG - ANNIE THINKS THE WORLD OF HIM - AND, AS FAR AS THAT GOES, YOU AND I ARE PRETTY GOOD PALS, TOO - EH, SANDY?

ARF!

Sensitive Trixie

E-E-E-K! OH, MY STARS! YOU'RE ENOUGH TO DRIVE ONE INSANE!

ARF!

STICKING YOUR HEAD THROUGH THE CURTAINS TO LEER AT ONE - ALWAYS FOLLOWING ME AROUND - YOU GIVE ME THE JITTERS - GET OUT! LEAVE ME ALONE - SCRAM!

GREAT SCOTT! I DON'T CARE HOW WONDERFUL THAT KID AND OLIVER THINK HE IS - HE'S GOING TO GO - THEY DON'T KNOW IT AND NEITHER DOES HE, BUT HE IS -

I'VE GOT TO BE CAREFUL - BUT I CAN WORK IT - I'LL TAKE HIM TO THE DOG-POUND AND SLIP THE MAN A FIVE TO SEE THAT THE BRUTE DOESN'T COME BACK - ALL I'LL HAVE TO DO IS SAY THE DOG GOT LOST IN THE CROWD - THEY'LL NEVER SUSPECT ME; AND, IF THEY SHOULD, THEY CAN'T PROVE A THING -

31

Outvoted

SAINTS ABOVE! THERE HE GOES— JUST THE MERE SIGHT OF THAT BRUTE GIVES ME THE JITTERS! HE'S UN-CANNY— THERE I TOOK HIM TO THE DOG-POUND YESTERDAY AND TURNED HIM OVER TO THE DOG-CATCHER—

AND I GAVE THE MAN FIVE DOLLARS AND HE PROMISED TO GET RID OF THE UGLY LUMMOX— YOU'D THINK THAT WOULD END IT— BUT WHEN I GOT HOME HERE, THE SHAGGY OAF WAS HERE AHEAD OF ME—

EEK! GET AWAY FROM ME— GET OUT! SCAT! DO YOU HEAR?

I THINK HE TAKES A FIENDISH DELIGHT IN STARTLING ME— HOW ON EARTH DID HE ESCAPE FROM THE DOG-POUND YESTERDAY? AND HOW DID HE GET ALL THE WAY BACK HERE SO QUICKLY? HE'S NOT NATURAL— IF I CAN'T GET RID OF HIM SOON, HE'LL DRIVE ME GOOFY—

HAROLD GRAY

Reg. U. S. Pat. Off.; Copyright, 1932, by The Chicago Tribune.

The Plot

HELLO, BILL— HOW ARE YOU? SURE GLAD TO SEE YOU, AREN'T WE, SANDY?

ARF!

HELLO, ANNIE— I JUST CAME UP TO SEE YOUR "DADDY"— I NEED HIS ADVICE ON A LITTLE BUSINESS MATTER—

HEY, "DADDY"! BILL'S HERE TO SEE YOU— ARE YOU BUSY?

BUSY? I SHOULD SAY NOT— COME ON IN, BILL—

DIDN'T I HEAR SOME ONE COME IN JUST NOW? WHO WAS IT, ANNIE?

JUST BILL TO SEE "DADDY"— YOU SEE THEIR OFFICES ARE JUST BELOW US IN THIS SAME BUILDING— BILL HAS AN APARTMENT RIGHT NEXT TO HIS OFFICE AND HE COMES UP OFTEN—

HOW I DESPISE THAT UGLY LITTLE RUNT— WHY DOES HE HAVE TO BE AROUND HERE SO MUCH? OLIVER HAS SUCH UNCOUTH FRIENDS— WHY CAN'T HE PICK FRIENDS WITH LEGS THE RIGHT SIZE? IT GIVES ME THE CREEPS JUST TO LOOK AT HIM—

HAROLD GRAY

Reg. U. S. Pat. Off.; Copyright, 1932, by The Chicago Tribune.

Bill Must Go

WELL, YOU SEE, BILL WAS AWFUL KIND TO "DADDY" WHEN "DADDY" WAS IN TROUBLE— SO NOW BILL IS "DADDY'S" PARTNER—

YES, I KNOW ALL ABOUT THAT, BUT WHY IS IT NECESSARY FOR THEM TO LIVE SO CLOSE TO-GETHER? WHY DOES BILL NEED TO LIVE RIGHT IN THE SAME BUILDING?

OH, HE DOESN'T NEED TO, I GUESS— BUT IT'S HANDY FOR HIM— HIS APARTMENT IS RIGHT NEXT DOOR TO HIS OFFICE— AND HE LIKES TO DROP IN HERE AND SEE "DADDY"—

OH, BILL MUST BE A WONDERFUL FELLOW— WHAT A SHAME HE IS A CRIPPLE—

WONDERFUL FELLOW, MY EYE! THE LITTLE GNOME— BUT I DON'T DARE SPEAK MY MIND IN FRONT OF THAT RED HEADED MINX— SHE'D TATTLE RIGHT TO OLIVER— I'VE GOT TO DOPE THIS OUT ALONE AND TELL NO ONE—

HUH— THAT LITTLE SCOTCH TERRIER ON HIS BANDY LEGS— POPPING IN AND OUT OF HERE TWENTY TIMES A DAY— WONDER WHAT HE AND OLIVER TALK ABOUT— IT'S A CINCH BILL DISLIKES ME— I CAN TELL— WELL, I'VE GOT TO FIND A WAY TO GET RID OF HIM— HM-M-M— I'LL BET HE'S TOUCHY— MOST BIRDS LIKE THAT ARE— I THINK I KNOW WHAT WILL FIX HIM—

HAROLD GRAY

Reg. U. S. Pat. Off.; Copyright, 1932, by The Chicago Tribune.

Trixie Finds His Weakness

His Move

Why, the Idea!

Indestructible Sandy

OH! THAT UNCANNY IMP OF SATAN! EVERY TIME I LOOK AROUND, THERE HE IS LEERING AT ME— CAN I NEVER BE RID OF HIM? ALL MY PLANS FAIL WHERE HE IS CONCERNED— AND I MUST KEEP ON PRETENDING THAT I LIKE THE UGLY MONGREL—

THERE— AT LEAST I'LL BE RID OF HIM FOR A FEW MINUTES— I THOUGHT SURELY I HAD SUCCEEDED YESTERDAY— I GAVE THOSE TWO THUGS FIFTY DOLLARS AND THEY DRAGGED SANDY INTO THEIR BOAT—

WHEN THEY WERE WAY OUT IN THE HARBOR THEY PUT HIM IN A SACK, WEIGHTED WITH ROCKS, AND THREW HIM IN WHERE THE WATER WAS TWO HUNDRED FEET DEEP— THEN THEY CALLED ME UP AND TOLD ME IT WAS ALL OVER— I WAS SO RELIEVED—

BUT I'D HARDLY HUNG UP THE 'PHONE TILL IN WALKED THAT FIENDISH LUMMOX, STILL SOAKING WET— HOW DID HE DO IT? IS THERE NO WAY TO LOSE HIM? BR·R·R·R! JUST THINKING ABOUT HIM GIVES ME THE SHIVERS—

HAROLD GRAY

Reg. U S Pat. Off., Copyright, 1932, by The Chicago Tribune.

The Chinese Retreat in Good Order

HUH! THERE COMES THAT AWFUL CHINAMAN TO SEE OLIVER— WHY MUST OLIVER HAVE SUCH TERRIBLE PEOPLE ABOUT ALL THE TIME? WELL, I GOT RID OF THAT UGLY DWARF— I MUST THINK OF SOME WAY TO GET RID OF THIS WUN WEY PERSON.

HOW DO YOU DO, MR. WUN WEY— OLIVER SAID YOU HAD AN APPOINTMENT WITH HIM HERE— I'M SURE HE'LL BE BACK IN A VERY FEW MINUTES— WON'T YOU WAIT?

THANK YOU, MRS. WARBUCKS— I HOPE I AM NOT INTRUDING—

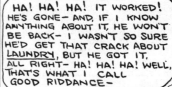

NOT AT ALL— BUT PLEASE PARDON ME— I WAS JUST REMINDED THAT WE HAVE BEEN HAVING TROUBLE WITH OUR LAUNDRY— I MUST GO AND ATTEND TO THE MATTER AT ONCE—

AH? QUITE SO— ON SECOND THOUGHT I DO NOT BELIEVE I WILL WAIT— PLEASE INFORM MR. WARBUCKS THAT I WAS HERE—

HA! HA! HA! IT WORKED! HE'S GONE— AND, IF I KNOW ANYTHING ABOUT IT, HE WON'T BE BACK— I WASN'T SO SURE HE'D GET THAT CRACK ABOUT LAUNDRY, BUT HE GOT IT, ALL RIGHT— HA! HA! HA! WELL, THAT'S WHAT I CALL GOOD RIDDANCE—

HAROLD GRAY

Reg. U. S. Pat. Off., Copyright, 1932, by The Chicago Tribune.

Oriental Logic

WHAT WAS YOUR HURRY, YESTERDAY? WHY DIDN'T YOU WAIT FOR ME? THE WIFE SAID YOU HAD BEEN GONE LESS THAN FIVE MINUTES WHEN I CAME IN—

TO BE QUITE FRANK, OLIVER, I DO NOT FEEL THAT MY PRESENCE IS DESIRABLE TO MRS. WARBUCKS—

NONSENSE, WUN WEY— WHY, SHE'S CRAZY ABOUT YOU— SHE COULDN'T UNDERSTAND WHY YOU LEFT SO ABRUPTLY—

I REGRET MOST DEEPLY ANY ANXIETY I MAY HAVE CAUSED MRS. WARBUCKS— BUT BUSINESS HERE IS MOST PRESSING— IT IS BEST THAT I REMAIN HERE CONSTANTLY— BUT I WILL BE MOST HAPPY TO SEE YOU HERE AT ANY TIME—

CONFOUND HIS ORIENTAL POLITENESS— WHY DOESN'T HE BLURT OUT WHAT'S THE MATTER? HE DOESN'T HAVE TO BE AFRAID OF HURTING MY FEELINGS— OUR FRIENDSHIP IS TOO STRONG TO BE WRECKED BY ANYTHING HE COULD SAY— BUSINESS, MY EYE! IT'S NOT THAT— HE JUST DOESN'T WANT TO COME TO MY PLACE— BUT WHY?

OLIVER IS MY DEAR FRIEND— HE IS ONE MAN IN TEN MILLION— TO ALL BUT HIM, HIS WIFE IS MOST COMMON TRASH, YET HE ADORES HER— WHY SHOULD I STOOP TO DESTROY HIS ILLUSION IN ORDER TO SOOTHE MY INJURED PRIDE? SHE DISLIKES ME— BUT IS THE ILL-WILL OF AN ILL-BRED CAT OF ANY CONSEQUENCE?

HAROLD GRAY

Reg. U. S. Pat. Off., Copyright, 1932, by The Chicago Tribune.

Telling the Lady

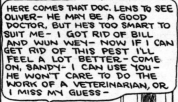

HERE COMES THAT DOC. LENS TO SEE OLIVER— HE MAY BE A GOOD DOCTOR, BUT HE'S TOO SMART TO SUIT ME— I GOT RID OF BILL AND WUN WEY— NOW IF I CAN GET RID OF THIS PEST I'LL FEEL A LOT BETTER— COME ON, SANDY— I CAN USE YOU— HE WON'T CARE TO DO THE WORK OF A VETERINARIAN, OR I MISS MY GUESS—

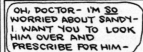

OH, DOCTOR— I'M SO WORRIED ABOUT SANDY— I WANT YOU TO LOOK HIM OVER AND PRESCRIBE FOR HIM—

CERTAINLY— HERE, SANDY, OLD FELLOW— LET'S SEE HOW YOUR PULSE IS— HM-M-M WHY, YOU SEEM QUITE NORMAL IN EVERY WAY—

ANNIE IS SO FOND OF SANDY— I'D HATE TO HAVE ANYTHING HAPPEN TO HIM— OF COURSE, HE IS ONLY A COMMON MONGREL—

SANDY MAY NOT HAVE A PEDIGREE, BUT HE HAS FAR MORE APPARENT BREEDING THAN SOME PEOPLE I HAVE KNOWN—

WELL! OF ALL THE NERVE! HOW DOES HE DARE TO TALK TO ME LIKE THAT— HE PRACTICALLY TELLS ME TO MY FACE THAT I HAVE LESS BREEDING THAN A MONGREL— AND HE WALKS OUT BEFORE I CAN THINK OF A THING TO SAY—

Reg. U. S. Pat. Off.; Copyright, 1932, by The Chicago Tribune.

Company Coming

GEE— IT'S SORTA LONESOME AROUND HERE— COURSE THERE'S TRIXIE— BUT SHE'S ALWAYS READIN' A BOOK OR JUST SITTIN' EATIN' CANDY— THERE'S NEVER MUCH GOIN' ON—

SAY, "DADDY"— I HAVEN'T SEEN BILL FOR A WEEK— HE USED TO COME IN EVERY DAY— AND WUN WEY HASN'T BEEN HERE SINCE TUESDAY— AND DOC. LENS WAS IN YESTERDAY, BUT HE STAYED ONLY A MINUTE— WHY DON'T THEY COME ANY MORE?

OH, THEY JUST HAPPEN TO BE BUSY, I GUESS— THEY'LL ALL BE AROUND AGAIN— I'LL HAVE THEM ALL IN TO DINNER SOME EVENING SOON—

WHAT IS IT, OTTO?

A RADIOGRAM FOR YOU, SIR— HIT HARRIVED JUST NOW, SIR—

WELL, WHAT DO YOU THINK OF THIS, ANNIE? THIS IS NEWS— A RADIOGRAM FROM GOOD OLD SPIKE MARLIN— HE'LL BE HERE MONDAY— HE'S TAKING A PLANE AS SOON AS HIS BOAT LANDS—

GEE— IT SURE WILL BE SWELL TO SEE CAP'N MARLIN AFTER ALL THESE MONTHS—

Reg. U. S. Pat. Off.; Copyright, 1932, by The Chicago Tribune

She's All a-Twitter

TELL ME, OLIVER— JUST WHO IS THIS CAPTAIN MARLIN, WHO IS GOING TO GET HERE MONDAY?

SPIKE MARLIN? WHY HE'S NOW HEAD OF MY SHIPPING COMPANY IN THE ORIENT— HE'S A REGULAR OLD SEA DOG— YOU'LL LIKE HIM IMMENSELY—

THIS CAPTAIN MARLIN MUST BE A WONDERFUL CHARACTER— I SUPPOSE YOU KNOW ALL ABOUT HIM—

SURE— HE'S A SWELL GUY— HE'S BEEN ALL OVER TH' WORLD— HE'S SPENT HIS WHOLE LIFE AT SEA— HE'S BEEN SHIP-WRECKED DOZENS O' TIMES— HE CAN TELL TH' GRANDEST STORIES, ALL ABOUT CANNIBALS AN' SHARKS AN' TYPHOONS AN' EVERTHING—

I GUESS THERE'S NOTHIN' HE DOESN'T KNOW ABOUT SHIPS— HE'S BEEN A SAILOR EVER SINCE HE WAS A LITTLE BOY— AND HE'S BEEN PLACES I'VE NEVER EVEN HEARD OF—

MY, HE MUST HAVE HAD A WONDERFUL LIFE— I'VE ALWAYS WANTED TO TRAVEL AND SEE THE WORLD— WE MUST GET HIM TO TALK OF HIS EXPERIENCES—

I WONDER HOW OLD HE IS AND WHAT HE LOOKS LIKE— I'LL BET HE'S A BIG, HANDSOME FELLOW— I'VE ALWAYS WANTED TO MEET A REAL SEA-CAPTAIN— THERE'S SOMETHING SO ROMANTIC ABOUT A SAILOR— I CAN HARDLY WAIT TO MEET HIM—

Reg. U. S. Pat. Off.; Copyright, 1932, by The Chicago Tribune

Here Comes a Sailor

Meet the Missus

A Head for Business

38

So Sorry

OH, IT'S JUST A LITTLE GET-TOGETHER, DOC.- YOU AND BILL AND WUN WEY- TRIXIE AND I WANT YOU BOYS TO COME AS EARLY AS YOU CAN- SPIKE MARLIN IS HERE AND THE PARTY'S FOR HIM- HE'S A GREAT CHAP- BEEN A SAILOR ALL HIS LIFE- GREATEST STORY-TELLER YOU EVER HEARD- OH- YOU CAN'T MAKE IT? SAY, THAT'S TOO BAD- OH, SURE- I UNDERSTAND- AWFULLY SORRY, THOUGH- TRIXIE AND I HAD COUNTED ON YOU-

WELL, YOU SEE, WUN WEY, SPIKE MARLIN IS HERE FROM THE FAR EAST FOR A FEW DAYS- I THOUGHT MAYBE YOU AND BILL WOULD LIKE TO MEET HIM- I'VE TOLD YOU ABOUT HIM AND HE'S ANXIOUS TO MEET YOU- DOC. LENS WOULD BE OVER, BUT HE CAN'T MAKE IT- TRIXIE'S COUNTING ON YOU- YOU CAN'T? YOU SAY YOU HAVE TO GO OUT OF TOWN? CAN'T PUT IT OFF, EH? MIGHTY SORRY- SURE- I KNOW YOU'D COME IF YOU COULD-

WHAT'S THAT, BILL? YOU'VE PROMISED TO BE GOD-FATHER AT A CHRISTENING TO-MORROW? OH, SURE- OF COURSE YOU CAN'T BREAK A DATE LIKE THAT- TRIXIE AND I HAD COUNTED ON YOU- OH, IT WAS TO BE JUST A LITTLE DINNER HERE FOR SPIKE MARLIN AND A TALK-FEST AFTERWARD- SURE- HE'LL BE IN TOWN FOR A COUPLE OF DAYS MORE- WE'LL GET TO-GETHER AT THE OFFICE-

THAT'S FUNNY- DOC. LENS, WUN WEY, BILL- NOT ONE OF THEM CAN COME- AND I'D FIGURED THEY'D ALL BE HERE- OH, WELL- SPIKE AND I CAN HAVE A GOOD VISIT AND I'LL GET HIM TO SPIN YARNS OF THE SEA- TRIXIE'LL LOVE THAT-

HAROLD GRAY

Reg. U. S. Pat. Off., Copyright, 1932, by The Chicago Tribune

A Cold Audience

AYE, FOR FORTY YEARS AND MORE, MAN AND BOY, I'VE SAILED THE SEVEN SEAS- I'VE SEEN SOME STRANGE PLACES AND SOME STRANGE SIGHTS- AYE, AND SOME STRANGER FOLK- THAT I HAVE-

YOU'VE NEVER HEARD THE ONE SPIKE TELLS ABOUT THE THREE MERMAIDS HE SAW ONE MOONLIT NIGHT TWO THOUSAND MILES OUT IN THE PACIFIC WHEN HE WAS BOUND FOR SYDNEY YEARS AGO- YOU'LL LIKE THIS ONE AND HE SWEARS IT'S TRUE-

AYE- TRUE AS GOSPEL-

THOSE WERE THE DAYS BEFORE EVERYTHING WAS STEAM OR OIL- GREAT SAILING SHIPS WE HAD, WITH REAL SAILOR-MEN TO MAN THEM- BUT I'M AFRAID THE MISSUS IS TIRED-

OH, I'M SO SORRY- BUT I HAVE A SPLITTING HEADACHE- I'M SURE YOU WILL EXCUSE ME IF I RETIRE EARLY-

HAROLD GRAY

Reg. U. S. Pat. Off.; Copyright, 1932, by The Chicago Tribune

Good-By, Sailor

HUMPH! THAT BIG WALRUS- I SAW HER SNEERING AT ME- YAWNING IN MY FACE- THE DUMB SEA-COW- WELL, I DON'T HAVE TO STAY UNDER THE SAME ROOF WITH HER ANY LONGER AND I'M DRAGGIN' MY ANCHOR- POOR WARBUCKS- BUT WE ALL MAKE MISTAKES-

SPIKE! WHERE ON EARTH ARE YOU GOING? I THOUGHT YOU WERE GOING TO STAY HERE WITH US WHILE YOU WERE IN TOWN-

I RECKON I'LL JUST RUN OUT TO THE LITTLE COTTAGE ON THE SHORE AND HAVE A LOOK AROUND- I WANT TO SEE THAT EVERYTHING THERE IS SHIP-SHAPE-

BUT, SPIKE- THE MISSUS WILL MISS YOU AS MUCH AS I WILL- AND THAT COTTAGE HAS BEEN CLOSED SINCE YOU WENT AWAY OVER A YEAR AGO-

OH, I'LL BE SNUG THERE, OLIVER- I WANT TO GET SOME OF MY THINGS FROM THERE BEFORE I GO BACK TO SINGAPORE- I'LL SEE YOU AGAIN BEFORE I LEAVE-

NOW WHAT COULD HAVE COME OVER HIM? IS THERE SOMETHING THE MATTER WITH THIS PLACE? DOC. AND BILL AND WUN WEY DON'T COME HERE ANY MORE- AND NOW SPIKE RUNS OUT LIKE HE'D BEEN SHOT AT AND MISSED- I WONDER-

HAROLD GRAY

Reg. U. S. Pat. Off.; Copyright, 1932, by The Chicago Tribune

40

The Baleful Eye

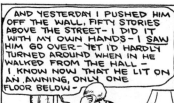

Strange Behavior

Till We Meet Again

41

Sandy Knows Something

He's Still Blind

Something for Sandy, Too

43

Safe All Around

Dawning Understanding

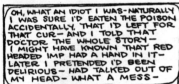

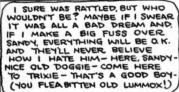

A Complicated Problem

His Pals

Walking It Off

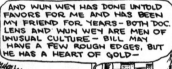

The New Interest

Miss Pish and Mr. Twiddle

BUT, MR. TWIDDLE - IT'S SUCH A PROBLEM TO KNOW WHERE TO BEGIN AND WHERE TO STOP -

AH, MY DEAR MRS. WARBUCKS - THERE CAN BE NO HALF-WAY MEASURES, IF YOU WOULD BE TRULY MODERN - DRAPES, WALLS, FURNITURE - ALL MUST BE IN TUNE -

AH, I UNDERSTAND YOUR HUSBAND FURNISHED THIS PLACE - WHAT A SHAME - A MAN CAN BE SOLD ANYTHING - BUT WE WOMEN DEMAND GRACE, BEAUTY, HARMONY -

JUST SO - NOW THESE CHAIRS - COMFORTABLE, NO DOUBT, BUT SO BOURGEOIS - THE LAMPS, TABLES, RUGS, EVERYTHING MUST GO, OF COURSE -

THAT PAINTING, FOR INSTANCE - BY A FAMOUS ARTIST - QUITE THE THING A FEW YEARS AGO - BUT NOT TO BE THOUGHT OF IN A TRULY MODERN HOME - OH, DEAR NO - NOT AT ALL -

MISS PISH AND MR. TWIDDLE, THE INTERIOR DECORATORS, ARE SURE GIVIN' TH' PLACE TH' ONCE OVER - ARE YOU GOIN' TO HAVE TH' HOUSE ALL RE-DECORATED?

HUH- WHAT'S THAT, ANNIE? OH, YES - I BELIEVE YOUR MOTHER IS CONSIDERING SOMETHING OF THE SORT -

All Pro and No Con

HI 'OPE YOU 'AVE A PLEASANT TRIP, SIR -

THANKS, PERKINS - GOOD-BYE -

HIT'S A BLINKIN' SHAME, HI CALLS HIT - RUNNING HIM OUT OF HIS OWN 'OUSE -

'E CAN'T STAND THAT MISS PISH AND MR. TWIDDLE, 'E CAN'T -

AND NO MORE CAN HI -

SH-H-H. HI 'EAR FOOT-STEPS HAPPROACHING -

HIT'S ALL THE MADAM'S DOING - HIT'S A GORGEOUS 'OME, BUT SHE WON'T BE 'APPY TILL SHE'S MADE A BLARSTED 'ORROR OUT OF IT -

HELLO - GO RIGHT ON TALKING - DON'T MIND ME -

HIT'S H'ALL RIGHT - SHE'S A JOLLY PRINCESS, SHE IS -

ALWAYS A SMILE AND A KIND WORD -

A BLOOMIN' BAD BREAK, HIT WAS FOR ER WHEN TH' MARSTER MARRIED THE MADAM -

A BAD BREAK FOR HALL OF US, HI SHOULD SAY -

Another Refugee

DOG GONE IT - I DON'T BLAME "DADDY" FOR GOIN' ON A TRIP - THIS IS A MESS, WITH PAINTERS AND WORKMEN SWARMING ALL OVER THE PLACE AND POPPING OUT AT YUH FROM EVERY DOOR-WAY - I'M GOIN' FOR A WALK -

SHUX - WHY DID TRIXIE HAVE TO GO AN' TEAR UP EVERYTHING? TH' WHOLE PLACE WAS FURNISHED BRAND NEW LESS'N A YEAR AGO, AND EVERYTHING THE VERY BEST - NOW SHE'S TOSSIN' EVER'THING OUT AN' STARTIN' ALL OVER - I GUESS SOME FOLKS JUST CAN'T BE SATISFIED 'LESS THEY'RE CHANGIN' THINGS -

"DADDY" WAS AWFUL SORE - COURSE HE DIDN'T SAY MUCH, BUT I COULD TELL - HE'S GOT MIGHTY GOOD SELF-CONTROL, BUT HE'S GOT A TERRIBLE TEMPER, TOO - GUESS HE FIGGERED HE COULDN'T HOLD IN MUCH LONGER, SO HE WANTED TO GET OUT WHERE HE'D HAVE PLENTY OF ROOM 'FORE HE BLEW UP -

Watt's That?

Progress

Surprise for "Daddy"

The Master's Voice

HERE I COME HOME AND FIND MY ROOM FULL OF A LOT OF CRAZY FURNITURE AND ALL OF MY STUFF MOVED OUT- THIS ROOM IS MINE- I'LL FURNISH IT AS I PLEASE AND I'LL STAND FOR NOBODY MOVING MY STUFF AROUND- AND I WANT MY STUFF ALL BACK NOW-

BUT, MY DEAR FELLOW- I FEAR THAT WILL BE QUITE IMPOSSIBLE- YOU SEE MRS. WARBUCKS TOLD US WE WERE TO HAVE WHAT THE OLD JUNK WOULD BRING FOR GETTING RID OF IT-

DO YOU MEAN TO SAY SHE GAVE YOU ALL OUR FURNITURE ON TOP OF PAYING YOU YOUR COMMISSION?

LISTEN, YOU- I'M NOT YOUR "DEAR FELLOW"- AND THAT FURNITURE WAS NOT "JUNK"- THE STUFF IN MY ROOM IS MY FURNITURE AND I DIDN'T GIVE IT TO YOU- BUT IF YOU DON'T HAVE IT BACK HERE IN JUST ONE HOUR I'VE GOT SOMETHING ELSE I'LL GIVE YOU, RIGHT ON THE NOSE! IS THAT CLEAR?

YES SIR, MR. WARBUCKS, I UNDERSTAND PERFECTLY NOW, MR. WARBUCKS-

ONE HOUR! OR I'LL NAIL YOUR HIDE ON A DOOR- REMEMBER!

GEE- I KNEW THOSE TWO SHARP-SHOOTERS WOULD CROWD THEIR LUCK TOO FAR- "DADDY" CAN BE PUSHED JUST SO FAR-

4-25

HAROLD GRAY

Reg. U.S. Pat. Off.; Copyright, 1932, by The Chicago Tribune.

Peace Declared

B-B-BUT OLIVER- I THOUGHT YOU'D LIKE IT- BOO-HOO-HOO!

THERE- THERE- TRIXIE- I'M SORRY- I DIDN'T MEAN TO LOSE MY TEMPER-

I SHOULD HAVE MADE THEM LEAVE YOUR ROOM ALONE- I REALIZE THAT NOW-

WELL, IT'S ALL O.K. NOW- I HAVE MY FURNITURE ALL BACK IN MY ROOM- YOU HAVE THE REST OF THE PLACE FIXED UP LIKE YOU WANT IT- LET'S FORGET ALL ABOUT IT NOW- EH, TRIXIE?

WELL, I'M GLAD THE WAR'S OVER- TRIXIE HAS HAD HER OWN WAY WITH ALL THE HOUSE 'CEPT "DADDY'S" ROOM HERE- AND HE'S GOT THIS ROOM FURNISHED JUST LIKE HE LIKES IT-

IF TRIXIE HAD GOT AWAY WITH THAT ONE, THERE'S NO TELLING WHAT SHE'D HAVE TRIED NEXT- BUT CAN YOU IMAGINE "DADDY" LETTIN' HER, OR ANYBODY ELSE, BOSS HIM AROUND? GEE, WITH HIS TEMPER, I GUESS THERE'S NO DANGER OF "DADDY" EVER TURNIN' OUT TO BE A HEN-PECKED HUSBAND, EH, SANDY?

ARF!

4-26

HAROLD GRAY

Reg. U.S. Pat. Off.; Copyright, 1932, by The Chicago Tribune

An Idea

I STILL THINK TRIXIE HAS MADE A MESS OF THE REST OF THE HOUSE WITH HER BIZARRE IDEA OF MODERN DECORATION- BUT, WITH MY ROOM HERE TO RETREAT TO, I CAN STAND IT- AND I CAN'T BLAME TRIXIE SO MUCH-

SHE'S COOPED UP HERE WITH NO OUTSIDE INTERESTS- NATURALLY SHE'S BOUND TO FIND SOME OUTLET FOR HER ENERGIES- WHAT MORE NATURAL THAN RE-FURNISHING THE PLACE? BY GEORGE! I HAVE AN IDEA-

YES, SIR- JUST THE THING FOR HER- A BIG COUNTRY PLACE- PLENTY OF ROOM- EXERCISE- HORSES- GARDENS- GOLF- AND I KNOW JUST THE PLACE, TOO- I'LL GET ANNIE TO HELP ME WITH THIS-

ANNIE, I HAVE AN IDEA HOW WE CAN SURPRISE TRIXIE- CAN YOU BE READY EARLY IN THE MORNING TO DRIVE OUT INTO THE COUNTRY WITH ME?

SURE, "DADDY"- THAT'LL BE FUN- BUT WHAT'S THE SURPRISE GOIN' TO BE?

4-27

HAROLD GRAY

Reg. U.S. Pat. Off.; Copyright, 1932, by The Chicago Tribune

Wrap It Up

OH, "DADDY"- THIS IS A WONDERFUL PLACE - YOU CAN TELL THAT WITH JUST ONE LOOK-

YES, ANNIE - I BELIEVE THIS PLACE WILL DO VERY WELL- IT'S LARGE ENOUGH AND JUST A NICE DISTANCE FROM TOWN- AND IT HAS BEEN PLANNED VERY WELL-

THE HOUSE IS COMPLETELY MODERN, YET THE GARDENS ARE CHARMING AND APPEAR QUITE OLD - THE AGENT WAS TO HAVE MET US HERE - I CAN'T WAIT ANY LONGER-

YOU'RE NOT LEAVING SO SOON, ARE YOU, MR. WARBUCKS? I'M SORRY I WAS DELAYED - I PRESUME YOU HAVE LOOKED AROUND A BIT-

YES, I LOOKED AROUND. THIS PLACE SEEMS TO BE WHAT I WANT- HERE IS MY CHECK MADE OUT FOR THE PRICE YOU QUOTED ME- PLEASE SEND ALL THE PAPERS TO MY OFFICE AS SOON AS POSSIBLE - I'LL TAKE POSSESSION AT ONCE -

GREAT CAESAR'S GHOST! WHAT A MAN !!! NO STALLING! NO CHISELING! ONE LOOK AND HE'LL TAKE IT AND HE HANDS ME A CHECK IN FULL- HE SURE KNOWS WHAT HE WANTS AND HE GETS IT- NO WONDER HE'S A BIG SHOT-

HAROLD GRAY

A Satisfied Customer

WHAT A LAYOUT, SANDY- ACRES AND ACRES OF GARDENS- THIS PATH LEADS DOWN TO THE STABLES- "DADDY" SAYS WE HAVE TWENTY SADDLE HORSES DOWN THERE-

ISN'T HE A DANDY? SORRY THAT'S ALL THE SUGAR I HAVE WITH ME- NEXT TIME I'LL BRING YOU AN APPLE -

JUST LOOK AT THAT VIEW - MILES AND MILES OF WOODS AND LAKES - AND "DADDY" SAYS THE WOODS ARE FULL OF GAME AND THE LAKES ARE FULL OF FISH - GEE- I COULD BE HAPPY HERE FOREVER, IF I NEVER SAW THE CITY AGAIN -

HAROLD GRAY

WHAT DO YOU THINK OF IT ALL, ANNIE? DO YOU THINK TRIXIE WILL LIKE IT ?

OH, "DADDY"- IT'S JUST PERFECT- TRIXIE CAN'T HELP BUT LOVE IT-

Reg. U. S. Pat. Off., Copyright, 1932, by The Chicago Tribune.

Happy Anticipation

WHERE ARE YOU, ANNIE? AN-NIE!

HERE I AM, "DADDY"-

COME ON, ANNIE - IT'S TIME WE WERE STARTING BACK TO TOWN- TRIXIE WILL BE GETTING CURIOUS ABOUT WHAT WE'RE UP TO -

I'LL BE GLAD WHEN WE GET MOVED OUT HERE AND DON'T HAVE TO GO TO TOWN AT ALL, UNLESS WE FEEL LIKE IT- BUT THERE'S STILL A LOT TO BE DONE HERE - THE HOUSE IS BEING PUT IN ORDER INSIDE AND OUT - THERE ARE A THOUSAND DETAILS - AND EVERYTHING MUST BE PERFECT, BEFORE WE SPRING THE BIG SURPRISE ON TRIXIE -

GEE- IT SURE WILL BE A SWELL SURPRISE FOR HER - HOW MUCH LONGER BEFORE WE CAN TELL HER, "DADDY?"

OH, ABOUT ANOTHER WEEK, I GUESS- I HOPE SHE REALLY LIKES IT ALL- BUT, PSHAW! WHO COULD HELP LIKING A COUNTRY PLACE LIKE THIS, ESPECIALLY IN THE SPRING?

HAROLD GRAY

Reg. U. S. Pat. Off., Copyright, 1932, by The Chicago Tribune.

Cottage and Castle

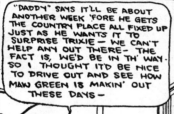

"DADDY" SAYS IT'LL BE ABOUT ANOTHER WEEK 'FORE HE GETS THE COUNTRY PLACE ALL FIXED UP JUST AS HE WANTS IT TO SURPRISE TRIXIE — WE CAN'T HELP ANY OUT THERE — THE FACT IS, WE'D BE IN TH' WAY — SO I THOUGHT IT'D BE NICE TO DRIVE OUT AND SEE HOW MAW GREEN IS MAKIN' OUT THESE DAYS —

5-2

WELL, KNOCK ME DOWN WITH A CROW-BAR IF IT AIN'T LITTLE ANNIE AND SANDY — HOW ARE YOU, ANYWAY?

HELLO, MAW GREEN — YOU DON'T WANT TO HIRE A FIRST-CLASS FARM-HAND FOR THAT JOB DO YOU?

OH, THINGS ARE GOING ALONG PRETTY GOOD — RIGHT NOW "DADDY" HAS BOUGHT A GORGEOUS COUNTRY ESTATE AND HE'S FIXIN' IT UP GRAND AS A PRESENT FOR TRIXIE —

COUNTRY ESTATE, EH? WELL, THAT'S FINE FOR SOME FOLKS — BUT GIVE ME A LITTLE COTTAGE WITH FLOWERS AND A GARDEN — A CAT, TO TALK TO AND FROGS TO SING TO ME — NO NOSEY NEIGHBORS — THIS IS THE LIFE FOR ME —

WHILE, IN THE MEANTIME, OUT AT THE GREAT COUNTRY ESTATE "DADDY" WORKS FEVERISHLY TO GET EVERYTHING IN PERFECT ORDER AGAINST TRIXIE'S ARRIVAL —

HAROLD GRAY

Reg. U.S. Pat. Off.; Copyright, 1932, by The Chicago Tribune.

Good Business

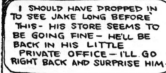

I SHOULD HAVE DROPPED IN TO SEE JAKE LONG BEFORE THIS — HIS STORE SEEMS TO BE GOING FINE — HE'LL BE BACK IN HIS LITTLE PRIVATE OFFICE — I'LL GO RIGHT BACK AND SURPRISE HIM —

5-3

HELLO, JAKE — HOW'S THINGS? ARE YOU BUSY?

YI-YI! LITTLE ANNIE! SO YOU HAVEN'T FORGOTTEN OLD JAKE — BUSY? YOU SHOULD ASK! JAKE WOULD NEVER BE TOO BUSY TO SEE YOU —

SO THE STORE IS GOING PRETTY WELL, EH?

WELL, IT COULD BE BETTER AND IT COULD BE WORSE — I BREAK EVEN — MAYBE A LITTLE MORE — IF I DIDN'T ADVERTISE, NOBODY WOULD COME TO BUY — BUT EVERY DAY IN THE PAPER I ADVERTISE AND I HOLD MY OWN — I COULDN'T COMPLAIN — AND YOU? HOW IS IT WITH YOU, NOW?

MEANWHILE, OUT AT THE NEW COUNTRY PLACE, "DADDY" BUYS ANOTHER DOZEN HORSES, FILLING HIS STABLES TO THE LAST STALL —

HAROLD GRAY

This and That

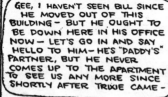

GEE, I HAVEN'T SEEN BILL SINCE HE MOVED OUT OF THIS BUILDING — BUT HE OUGHT TO BE DOWN HERE IN HIS OFFICE NOW — LET'S GO IN AND SAY HELLO TO HIM — HE'S "DADDY'S" PARTNER, BUT HE NEVER COMES UP TO THE APARTMENT TO SEE US ANY MORE SINCE SHORTLY AFTER TRIXIE CAME —

5-4

HELLO, BILL — I JUST THOUGHT I'D DROP IN AND SAY HELLO — "DADDY'S" OUT IN THE COUNTRY, YOU KNOW, AND IT'S SORT O' LONESOME WITHOUT HIM —

HELLO, ANNIE — YES, I HEARD ABOUT THE NEW COUNTRY PLACE — IT MUST BE A KNOCKOUT — I SUPPOSE YOU'LL BE MOVING OUT THERE SOON —

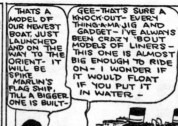

THAT'S A MODEL OF OUR NEWEST BOAT, JUST LAUNCHED AND ON THE WAY TO THE ORIENT — IT WILL BE SPIKE MARLIN'S FLAG SHIP, TILL A BIGGER ONE IS BUILT —

GEE — THAT'S SURE A KNOCK-OUT — EVERY THING-A-MA-JIG AND GADGET — I'VE ALWAYS BEEN CRAZY 'BOUT MODELS OF LINERS — THIS ONE IS ALMOST BIG ENOUGH TO RIDE ON — I WONDER IF IT WOULD FLOAT IF YOU PUT IT IN WATER —

WHILE, OVER THE ROADS TO THE COUNTRY ESTATE, ROLLS A FLEET OF TRUCKS, BRINGING FURNITURE AND RUGS AND EVERY FITTING TO CONVERT THE GREAT HOUSE INTO A SUMPTUOUS PALACE, JUST FOR TRIXIE —

HAROLD GRAY

Reg. U.S. Pat. Off.; Copyright, 1932, by The Chicago Tribune.

Here and There

SO YOU SHALL BE MOVING TO THE COUNTRY SOON — IT SHOULD BE VERY BEAUTIFUL THIS TIME OF YEAR —

YES, IT'S SWELL OUT THERE — AND THERE ARE HORSES TO RIDE AND THERE'S FISHING AND SWIMMING AND EVERYTHING — IT'S ALL TO BE A SURPRISE FOR TRIXIE — COURSE I'LL HATE TO LEAVE TOWN — BUT YOU AND BILL AND DOC. LENS MUST COME OUT AND VISIT US REAL OFTEN —

IF YOU GO TO THE COUNTRY YOU WILL NOT BE HERE TO BRIGHTEN MY HUMBLE SHOP WITH YOUR VISITS — BY THE WAY, I JUST RECEIVED SOME GOODS FROM CHINA — I PUT THIS SMALL TRINKET ASIDE FOR YOU — I HOPE YOU LIKE IT —

OH, WUN WEY — I COULDN'T TAKE IT — IT'S BEAUTIFUL, BUT IT'S LOTS TOO SWELL FOR ME — HONEST —

GEE — WUN WEY SURE IS A SWELL GUY — HE INSISTED THAT I TAKE THIS NECKLACE — I TRIED TO TELL HIM I DIDN'T WANT IT — BUT HE KNEW WELL ENOUGH NO GIRL COULD HELP WANTING A NECKLACE AS NICE AS THIS — "DADDY" SURE HAS THE BEST FRIENDS — I WISH THEY'D DROP IN TO VISIT US, LIKE THEY USED TO —

WHILE, OUT AT THE COUNTRY ESTATE, A GREAT, WALLED, FORMAL GARDEN HAS BEEN LAID OUT BELOW THE TERRACE — BLAZING WITH COLOR IT IS AN EXOTIC GEM IN A RUSTIC SETTING —

Hard Luck Trixie

I TELL YOU, GYPSY GAY, THIS MATRIMONY RACKET ISN'T ALL IT'S CRACKED UP TO BE BY A LONG SHOT — OLIVER HASN'T AN OUNCE OF TASTE — HE'S JUST AN OLD FOSSIL —

YEAH? WELL, I COULD FIND SOMETHING TO ADMIRE IN ANY MAN WHO HAS AS MANY BILLIONS AS YOUR OLIVER HAS — AND YOU ADMIT HE'S LIBERAL — HE NEVER KICKS ABOUT ANY BILL, NO MATTER HOW LARGE —

OH, I KNOW HE DOESN'T MIND WHAT I SPEND — THAT PART IS O. K. BUT THAT RED-HEADED BRAT AND HER MONGREL CUR — HONESTLY, SOMETIMES I THINK OLIVER CARES MORE FOR THEM THAN HE DOES FOR ME —

FIDDLESTICKS, TRIXIE — WHAT OF IT? YOU HAVE IT SOFT, HAVEN'T YOU? I'LL BET THOUSANDS OF WOMEN WOULD BE GLAD TO TRADE PLACES WITH YOU —

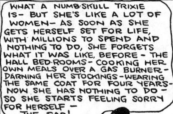

WHAT A NUMB-SKULL TRIXIE IS — BUT SHE'S LIKE A LOT OF WOMEN — AS SOON AS SHE GETS HERSELF SET FOR LIFE, WITH MILLIONS TO SPEND AND NOTHING TO DO, SHE FORGETS WHAT IT WAS LIKE, BEFORE — THE HALL BED-ROOMS — COOKING HER OWN MEALS OVER A GAS BURNER — DARNING HER STOCKINGS — WEARING THE SAME COAT FOR FOUR YEARS — NOW SHE HAS NOTHING TO DO — SO SHE STARTS FEELING SORRY FOR HERSELF — THE SAP!

WHILE AN ARMY OF SERVANTS INUNDATES THE GREAT COUNTRY PLACE, FILLING EVERY NOOK AND CORNER —

Final Touches

A LITTLE MORE THAT WAY, PHIL — THERE — THAT'S BETTER —

WELL, ANNIE — HOW DO YOU LIKE IT? DO YOU THINK TRIXIE WILL CARE FOR IT?

IT'S PERFECTLY GORGEOUS, "DADDY" — EVERYTHING IS PERFECT — SHE CAN'T HELP LIKING IT —

MY, ANNIE — YOU CERTAINLY HAVE A KNACK FOR ARRANGING FLOWERS — IT'S THE WOMAN'S TOUCH, I SUPPOSE —

OH, THERE'S NOTHING TO IT — YOU JUST MOVE 'EM AROUND TILL THEY LOOK RIGHT — THAT'S ALL —

WELL, I GUESS IT'S READY FOR HER — I CAN'T THINK OF ANYTHING MORE THAT I CAN DO — I HOPE SHE REALLY LIKES IT — I DO WANT TRIXIE TO BE HAPPY AND CONTENTED —

YOU DON'T HAVE TO WORRY ABOUT THAT, "DADDY" — ANYONE WOULD HAVE TO BE HAPPY IN A PLACE LIKE THIS —

54

Not a Street Car Was in Sight

Cooling Off

No Dice

My Wife's Gone to the City

Fate Tricks Trixie

Little Slam

58

You Must Come Over

She's All a-Twitter

Her Pals

59

No Hits

Your Friends and My Friends

The Actress

61

Where Ignorance Is Bliss

THERE GOES THAT UGLY LITTLE PEST— UGH— WHAT I WOULDN'T GIVE TO BE RID OF HER! WHAT OLIVER SEES IN HER IS MORE THAN I CAN UNDERSTAND— THE ILL-BRED LITTLE WRETCH IS ALWAYS STICKING HER NOSE INTO EVERYONE'S BUSINESS—

5-23

IF SHE WERE ANY RELATION TO OLIVER, IT WOULD BE DIFFERENT— BUT AN ORPHAN— A NAMELESS WAIF— IT'S INCREDIBLE— AND HERE I HAVE TO PUT UP WITH THE LITTLE SNIP AND PRETEND TO LIKE HER— IT'S ALMOST UNBEARABLE AT TIMES—

SOMETIMES TRIXIE GETS ON MY NERVES SOMETHING AWFUL— SHE'S SO NARROW ON SOME SUBJECTS— AND HER IDEAS ON FURNITURE— AND HER SHALLOW, HALF-BAKED FRIENDS—

BUT SHE LOVES ANNIE— FOR THAT REASON I'D PUT UP WITH ALMOST ANYTHING FROM HER— YES, SIR— ALMOST ANYTHING—

Just Supposing

HM-M-M— " ACCORDING TO THE WILL OF THE LATE ALEXANDER P. GOTROCKS, WHICH WAS ADMITTED TO PROBATE YESTERDAY, THE WIDOW IS BEQUEATHED TWENTY-TWO MILLIONS, MOSTLY IN GOVERNMENT BONDS— MRS. GOTROCKS WAS FORMERLY MISS PEARLIE PRATTLE OF MUSICAL COMEDY FAME—"

TWENTY-TWO MILLIONS— AND IN GOVERNMENT BONDS— AND SHE WAS A SHOW GIRL, TOO— HUM-M-M— OLIVER MUST BE WORTH BILLIONS— IF ANYTHING SHOULD HAPPEN—

5-24

OF COURSE, THERE'S THAT RED-HEADED LITTLE IMP- OLIVER IS A SAP IN SOME WAYS— THERE'S NO TELLING WHAT HE'D LEAVE HER— STILL, SHE'S ONLY AN ORPHAN— I WONDER IF OLIVER HAS MADE A WILL LATELY—

OF COURSE I DON'T WANT ANYTHING TO HAPPEN TO OLIVER— BUT JUST SUPPOSE WOW! WOULD I BE A SENSATION? WITH MY FIGURE AND A BILLION DOLLARS!

HAROLD GRAY

After All

LISTEN, OLIVER— MAYBE IT'S HARDLY A SUBJECT THAT SHOULD BE MENTIONED, BUT THESE DAYS ONE NEVER KNOWS WHAT WILL HAPPEN NEXT, AND AS YOUR WIFE, I THINK I HAVE A RIGHT TO KNOW— IF YOU HAVE MADE A WILL, WOULD YOU MIND TELLING ME WHAT PROVISION YOU HAVE MADE FOR ME?

5-25

THAT'S A FAIR AND SENSIBLE QUESTION, TRIXIE— SURE, I'VE MADE A WILL— IN CASE I MEET WITH AN ACCIDENT YOU GET HALF— AND LITTLE ANNIE GETS HALF—

WHAT? THAT WAIF? SHE'S NOT EVEN YOUR OWN CHILD- SHE'S NOBODY'S CHILD- BUT I AM YOUR LAWFULLY WEDDED WIFE— YET YOU MEAN TO SAY YOU HAVE LEFT HER THE SAME AMOUNT YOU HAVE LEFT ME?

SURE— WHAT'S SO WRONG WITH THAT? ISN'T HALF MY FORTUNE ENOUGH TO SUIT YOU? WOULDN'T IT BE ENOUGH FOR ANYONE?

WELL, IT'S MOST DECIDEDLY TOO MUCH FOR A SMART-ALECK LITTLE ORPHAN, LIKE ANNIE— SHE SHOULD BE IN A GOOD INSTITUTION—

WHAM!

HAROLD GRAY

62

Disillusioned

GREAT SCOTT! WHAT DOES THE WOMAN WANT? HALF MY FORTUNE WOULD AMOUNT TO BILLIONS - YET SHE FLIES INTO A RAGE, AS IF I HAD TRIED TO CHEAT HER - IT'S JEALOUSY, OF COURSE - THAT'S CLEAR ENOUGH - IT'S THE IDEA OF ANNIE GETTING AS MUCH AS SHE, THAT BURNS HER UP -

AND THE THINGS SHE CALLED ANNIE - OF COURSE, SHE WAS UPSET AND EXCITED - BUT IT'S PLAIN ENOUGH SHE WAS SPEAKING WHAT REALLY IS IN HER MIND, ABOUT THE CHILD - IF SHE HAD AN OUNCE OF LOVE FOR ANNIE, SHE COULD NEVER HAVE TALKED ABOUT HER LIKE THAT -

ALL THE TIME, I'VE BEEN SO SURE TRIXIE LOVED ANNIE - WHAT AN OLD FOOL I'VE BEEN - STILL, IF ANNIE CAN BE KEPT FROM FINDING OUT, IT WON'T BE SO BAD - I SUPPOSE I'M TO BLAME FOR THE WHOLE MESS - I THOUGHT I WAS SUCH A GREAT JUDGE OF CHARACTER - HUH!

I WONDER WHAT A REALLY SMART MAN WOULD DO IN A CASE LIKE THIS - I'D LIKE TO ASK WUN WEY'S ADVICE - HE'D KNOW WHAT WAS BEST - BUT ONE DOESN'T DISCUSS SUCH PERSONAL MATTERS, EVEN WITH ONE'S BEST FRIEND - IT JUST ISN'T DONE - NOPE, I'VE GOT TO DOPE THIS OUT BY MYSELF -

The Heir Apparent

IMAGINE - HALF HIS FORTUNE TO THAT RED-HEADED ORPHAN WRETCH - BUT ME, HIS OWN WIFE, I AM TO BE LEFT THE OTHER HALF - WHAT ON EARTH CAN HE BE THINKING OF? IT'S OUTRAGEOUS - UNJUST - UNFAIR - PREPOSTEROUS - I MUST DO SOMETHING - BUT WHAT? IT'S USELESS TO ARGUE WITH THE OLD NUMB-SKULL -

WHY, TRIXIE, DEAR - I SHOULD THINK YOU COULD BREAK A WILL LIKE THAT - THE CHILD IS ONLY AN ORPHAN -

NO, I'M AFRAID THAT WOULDN'T WORK - FROM WHAT I'VE HEARD ABOUT WARBUCKS, HIS LAWYERS NEVER MAKE ANY MISTAKES - TEN TO ONE YOU'D NEVER GET TO FIRST BASE BREAKING A WILL OF HIS -

BUT THERE MUST BE SOMETHING I CAN DO - IMAGINE - THAT CHILD, STANDING BETWEEN ME AND BILLIONS - IT'S UNTHINKABLE - SHE SHOULD BE IN AN ORPHAN ASYLUM - BELIEVE ME, IF I HAD MY WAY, I'D HAVE HER IN AN INSTITUTION THIS MINUTE - BUT OLIVER THINKS SHE'S WONDERFUL - SO UNSPOILED AND SWEET - HE MUST BE SOFT IN THE HEAD -

WELL, TRIXIE, IF YOU ASK ME, I THINK YOU'RE SOFT IN THE HEAD - WHAT ARE YOU KICKING ABOUT? TO BEGIN WITH, YOUR OLIVER IS THE LIVEST GUY I EVER SAW - HE MAY LIVE FIFTY YEARS YET - AND WHAT IF THE KID SHOULD GET A LOT OF DOUGH? YOU'D GET BILLIONS, WOULDN'T YOU? WHY WANT IT ALL? YOU'RE SITTING PRETTY - MY ADVICE TO YOU IS TO SIT TIGHT AND DON'T ROCK THE BOAT -

A House Divided

HURRY UP, ANNIE - ARE YOU ABOUT READY TO START? THE CAR'S WAITING - WE WANT TO GET OUT TO THE COUNTRY IN TIME TO TAKE THAT LONG HORSE-BACK RIDE WE PLANNED -

WHERE'S TRIXIE? AREN'T WE GOING TO WAIT FOR HER?

TRIXIE'S NOT GOING OUT TO THE COUNTRY THIS WEEK-END - SHE'S GOING TO STAY IN TOWN - THERE'S A TEA OR SOMETHING SHE HAS TO ATTEND, I BELIEVE -

GEE, IT'S TOO BAD TRIXIE COULDN'T COME TOO - IT MUST HAVE BEEN SOMETHIN' AWFUL IMPORTANT THAT KEPT HER IN TOWN - I GUESS NOBODY WOULD MISS SPENDING THE WEEK-END IN THE COUNTRY THIS TIME O' YEAR IF THEY COULD HELP IT -

WELL, ANNIE SURE IS IN FINE SPIRITS, ANYWAY - I WISH I FELT HALF AS GOOD AS SHE DOES - BUT TRIXIE'S OUTBURST THE OTHER DAY GAVE ME A JOLT - I'M JUST AS WELL PLEASED THAT SHE STAYED IN TOWN THIS WEEK-END - IT WILL GIVE ME A CHANCE TO BE ALONE AND THINK THIS THING OUT -

C'MON, SANDY - LET'S HURRY DOWN AND SAY HELLO TO THE NEW COLT -

63

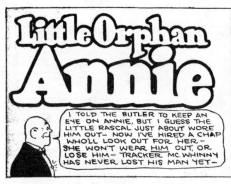

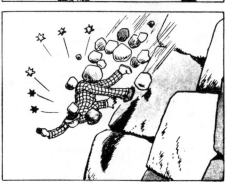

The Trust

The Trust Buster

Gone but Not Forgotten

What Has Happened to Justice?

Wun Wey X-Ray

The Country Calls

Was That the Human Thing to Do?

I'm Telling You

Contact

The Helping Hand

The Passport

Au Revoir

The Dreamer

Now Is the Time

The Little Promoter

Looking Ahead

The Thinker

A Dream Comes True

Partners

Wrap It Up

The Magic Skimmer

Tell Her Nothing

The Yellow Peril

When No One Pursueth

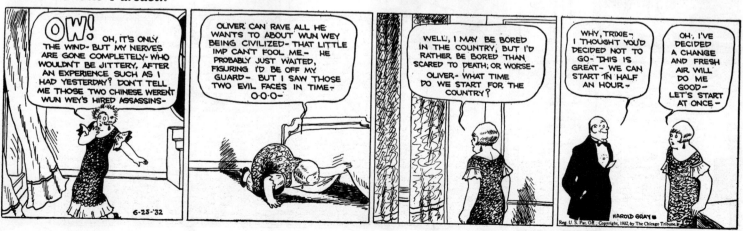

A-Shopping She Will Go

Shocking News

Her Worst Fears Confirmed

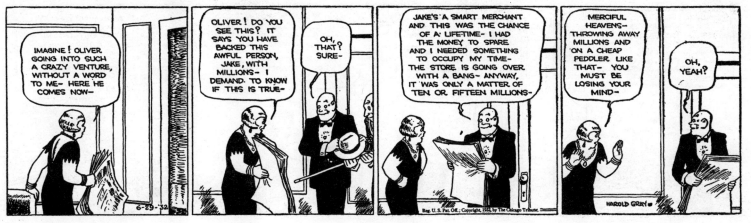

"I Want My Lawyer"

Timothy J. Jackal

Evidence

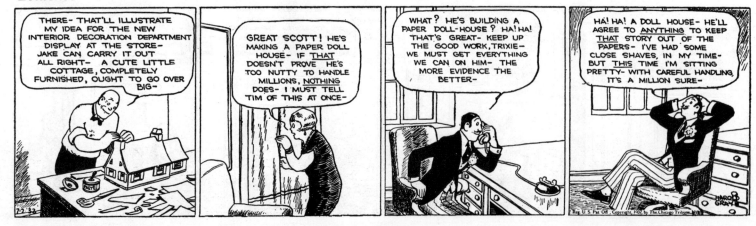

The Fireworks

Trixie Sulks

As Annie Dopes It Out

Preparing to Hop Off

Just for That

Happy Family

A Simple Plan

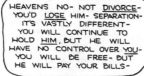

You Go Your Way

Her Mind Made Up

Watchful Annie

POOR "DADDY"- HE HAS HARDLY A WORD FOR ANYONE LATELY- HE'S BEEN PRETTY BUSY HELPING JAKE GET THE BIG, NEW STORE STARTED- HE MUST BE GOING TO THE STORE NOW-

LUCKY HE IS BUSY- IT KEEPS HIS MIND OFF O' OTHER THINGS-THE WAY TRIXIE TREATS HIM, HE'D BLOW UP, I BETCHA, IF HE DIDN'T HAVE LOTS O' OTHER THINGS TO THINK ABOUT-

NOW, WHERE TH' SAM HILL CAN SHE BE GOING? TRIXIE'S BEEN BUSIER HERE LATELY THAN A FLEA ON A HOT STOVE-

SHE'S BEEN ACTIN' LIKE SHE HAD A SECRET OR SOMETHIN' ON HER MIND- I'D GIVE A NICKEL TO KNOW WHAT SHE'S UP TO-

7-14-'32

Reg. U. S. Pat. Off.: Copyright, 1932, by The Chicago Tribune

It's in the Bag

DON'T WORRY FOR A SECOND, TRIXIE- IT WILL ALL BE ARRANGED MOST SIMPLY- YOU SHALL SEE-

BUT, TIM- ARE YOU SURE? I DON'T WANT ANY SLIP-UPS- YOU DON'T KNOW MY HUSBAND-

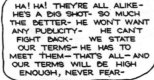

HA! HA! THEY'RE ALL ALIKE- HE'S A BIG SHOT- SO MUCH THE BETTER- HE WON'T WANT ANY PUBLICITY- HE CAN'T FIGHT BACK- WE STATE OUR TERMS- HE HAS TO MEET THEM- THAT'S ALL- AND OUR TERMS WILL BE HIGH ENOUGH, NEVER FEAR-

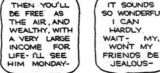

THEN YOU'LL BE FREE AS THE AIR, AND WEALTHY, WITH A VERY LARGE INCOME FOR LIFE- I'LL SEE HIM MONDAY-

IT SOUNDS SO WONDERFUL- I CAN HARDLY WAIT- MY, WON'T MY FRIENDS BE JEALOUS-

MONDAY I MEET THIS BIRD, WARBUCKS, AND GIVE HIM THE BAD NEWS- A FEW DAYS FOR HIM TO THINK IT OVER- THEN THE PAY-OFF AND EASY STREET- HOT DOG!!!

CLICK!

7-15-32

Reg. U. S. Pat. Off.; Copyright, 1932, by The Chicago Tribune

HAROLD GRAY

All Over but the Shouting

MY, THE WONDERFUL TRIPS I CAN TAKE, AS SOON AS TIM JACKAL, MY LAWYER, GETS MY SETTLEMENT FROM OLIVER- PARIS FIRST, OF COURSE, TO BUY GOWNS- THEN DEAUVILLE, BIARRITZ, THE WHOLE RIVIERA- WHAT A LIFE-

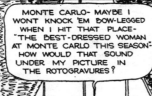

MONTE CARLO- MAYBE I WON'T KNOCK 'EM BOW-LEGGED WHEN I HIT THAT PLACE- "THE BEST-DRESSED WOMAN AT MONTE CARLO THIS SEASON"- HOW WOULD THAT SOUND UNDER MY PICTURE IN THE ROTOGRAVURES?

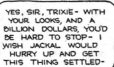

YES, SIR, TRIXIE- WITH YOUR LOOKS, AND A BILLION DOLLARS, YOU'D BE HARD TO STOP- I WISH JACKAL WOULD HURRY UP AND GET THIS THING SETTLED-

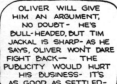

OLIVER WILL GIVE HIM AN ARGUMENT, NO DOUBT- HE'S BULL-HEADED, BUT TIM JACKAL IS SHARP- AS HE SAYS, OLIVER WON'T DARE FIGHT BACK- THE PUBLICITY WOULD HURT HIS BUSINESS- IT'S AS GOOD AS SETTLED-

7-16-32

Reg. U. S. Pat. Off.; Copyright, 1932, by The Chicago Tribune

HAROLD GRAY

85

Out of the Blue

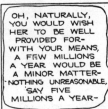

As One Man Sees It

Shellacking the Shyster

Or Else

Unsettled Trixie

Bon Voyage

The Break

The Patient Rests

The Doc Said REST

The Idea

O. K. Aloft

Great Expectations

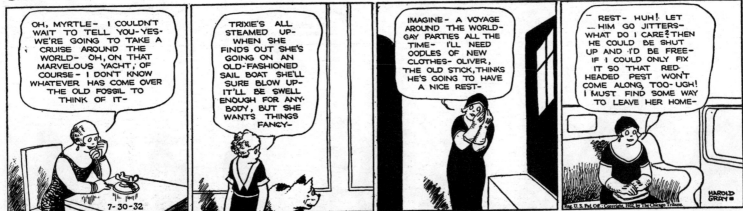

91

Great Minds

IF I GO ON THAT YACHT TRIP 'ROUND TH' WORLD, WITH "DADDY" AND TRIXIE, NOBODY WILL HAVE ANY FUN—

TRIXIE HATES ME AND I'D SPOIL TH' TRIP FOR HER, SO SHE'D SPOIL IT FOR "DADDY" AND, IF HE WASN'T HAPPY, I COULDN'T BE- GEE- I'VE GOTTA FIGGER OUT SOMETHIN'-

I WISH—- BUT WHAT'S THE USE? THERE'S NO WAY TO HELP IT- BUT TRIXIE AND ANNIE ON THE SAME BOAT FOR MONTHS- IT'LL BE A MAD-HOUSE IN A WEEK-

ANNIE CAN GET ALONG WITH ANYONE- IT'S NOT HER FAULT- WHY DO WE ALWAYS THINK OF MAKING CONCESSIONS TO PEOPLE WITH THE MOST EVIL TEMPERS? TRIXIE CAN LIKE IT OR LUMP IT- I WON'T SUGGEST LEAVING ANNIE BEHIND-

8-1-32

HAROLD GRAY

Reg. U. S. Pat. Off.; Copyright, 1932, by The Chicago Tribune

Trixie Votes YES!

"DADDY", I'VE BEEN THINKIN'- IT'D BE LOTS BETTER FOR EVERYBODY IF SANDY AND I DON'T GO ON THE YACHT TRIP WITH YOU AND TRIXIE- AND I WON'T MIND STAYIN' HOME-

NONSENSE ANNIE- WHATEVER PUT THAT IDEA INTO YOUR MIND?

BUT, "DADDY"- I'D GET ALONG FINE- I COULD GO TO A NICE BOARDIN' SCHOOL 'TILL YOU GOT BACK- I'D LIKE THAT-

A BOARDING SCHOOL, EH? HM-M-M- I HADN'T THOUGHT OF THAT- OH, TRIXIE- COME HERE A MINUTE-

YOU'D RATHER GO TO A NICE BOARDING SCHOOL, THAN TO GO ON THE YACHT? WHY, I THINK THAT WOULD BE WONDERFUL-

DO YOU KNOW OF ANY GOOD SCHOOLS FOR HER, TRIXIE?

OH, THERE ARE HUNDREDS OF MARVELOUS GIRLS' SCHOOLS- WE'LL PICK OUT THE VERY NICEST ONE- AND I'M SURE YOU'LL LIKE THAT MUCH MORE THAN THE OLD YACHT- I THINK THAT'S A PERFECTLY DELIGHTFUL IDEA-

8-2-

HAROLD GRAY

Reg. U. S. Pat. Off.; Copyright, 1932, by The Chicago Tribune

A Fateful Meeting

SO SHE WANTS TO PASS UP THE YACHT TRIP AND GO TO SCHOOL- TO THINK THAT SHE'D PLAY RIGHT INTO MY HANDS LIKE THAT-

TRIXIE! I MIGHT HAVE KNOWN IT, WHEN I SAW THAT SWELL CAR PULL UP- I HEARD YOU HAD MARRIED INTO THE BIG MONEY-

CLARA TREAT! IMAGINE MEETING YOU HERE, AND AFTER ALL THESE YEARS- WHAT ARE YOU DOING IN TOWN?

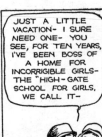

JUST A LITTLE VACATION- I SURE NEED ONE- YOU SEE, FOR TEN YEARS, I'VE BEEN BOSS OF A HOME FOR INCORRIGIBLE GIRLS- THE "HIGH-GATE SCHOOL FOR GIRLS, WE CALL IT-

YOU'D BE SURPRISED HOW MUCH THAT INTERESTS ME, CLARA- YOU SAY YOU CALL THIS PLACE A "SCHOOL"?

SURE- IT'S A SCHOOL, ALL RIGHT, AND MIGHTY STRICT- ONCE WE GET 'EM YOU CAN BE SURE WHERE THEY ARE AND THAT THEY'RE KEEPING BUSY-

CLARA- THIS MUST BE FATE- YOU CAN HELP ME AND BE PAID PLENTY- I'LL EXPLAIN EVERYTHING TO YOU AND TELL YOU JUST WHAT TO DO AND SAY- NOW LISTEN-

8-3-32

HAROLD GRAY

Reg. U. S. Pat. Off.; Copyright, 1932, by The Chicago Tribune

Helpful Trixie

HERE I AM, "DADDY:- I'M COMING-

COME IN, ANNIE- TRIXIE WANTS TO TELL YOU ABOUT THE SCHOOL SHE'S FOUND FOR YOU-

IT WAS JUST LIKE FATE, MEETING MISS TREAT- WHY, I'VE KNOWN CLARA SINCE WE WERE KIDS; THOUGH I HADN'T SEEN HER FOR TEN YEARS-

"HIGH-GATE SCHOOL FOR GIRLS," AND CLARA IS THE HEAD OF IT- ISN'T THAT WONDERFUL? CLARA SAYS IT'S A PERFECTLY CHARMING PLACE AND, KNOWING HER SO WELL, SHE'LL TAKE A SPECIAL INTEREST IN ANNIE AND GIVE HER MORE PERSONAL ATTENTION THAN SHE'D GET IN JUST ANY SCHOOL-

TRIXIE REALLY MEANS WELL- SHE'S NOT BAD AT HEART- LOOK AT THE INTEREST SHE'S TAKING IN FINDING ANNIE A REALLY FINE SCHOOL, WHERE SHE'LL BE WELL LOOKED AFTER-

Two Sweet Characters

I'VE HAD OLIVER FIX IT SO YOU'LL BE ABLE TO DRAW AS MUCH MONEY AS YOU WANT ANY TIME, IN YOUR OWN NAME- OF COURSE, HE THINKS IT'S ALL FOR ANNIE'S EXPENSES-

WHAT HE THINKS IS O.K. WITH ME- I SURE CAN USE SOME DOUGH- HOW HIGH CAN I GO?

THERE'S NO LIMIT, CLARA- HE'S A SAP WHERE THAT RED-HEADED PEST IS CONCERNED- WE WON'T BE BACK FOR A YEAR OR SO- ANYTHING CAN HAPPEN IN THAT TIME- SO DON'T WORRY- SPEND AS MUCH AS YOU LIKE-

YOU'RE SURE GIVING ME A BREAK, TRIXIE- DON'T WORRY- I'LL KEEP AN EYE ON THAT BRAT- SHE'LL NEVER SQUAWK, ONCE I GET HER INSIDE HIGH GATE "SCHOOL"-

SH! HERE THEY COME NOW-

THIS IS MISS TREAT, THE HEAD OF HIGH-GATE SCHOOL, AND MY OLD-TIME FRIEND-

AND THIS IS LITTLE ANNIE- MY- MY- WHAT A SWEET CHILD-

HOW DO YOU DO, MISS TREAT-

It Won't Be Long Now

WE COULD START TODAY, BUT OLIVER INSISTS ON WAITING TILL MONDAY-

MONDAY, EH? THEN I'LL FIGURE ON STARTING BACK WITH THE KID ON WEDNESDAY-

I SURE HOPE YOU HAVE A SWELL TIME ON YOUR TRIP, "DADDY"- YOU'LL BE GONE MOST A YEAR-

I WISH YOU WERE GOING TOO, ANNIE-

SHUX- I GOT ABOUT ENOUGH OCEAN, FOR A WHILE, WHEN I WAS SHIP-WRECKED ON THAT ISLAND- I'LL GET A KICK OUT OF GOING TO SCHOOL-

YES- THEY SAY THIS "HIGH-GATE SCHOOL" IS A NICE PLACE- I'M SURE YOU'LL LIKE IT THERE-

YES- MISS TREAT SAYS IT'S SWELL- SHE'S SORT O' FUNNY- BUT I GUESS IT'S JUST BEIN' A SCHOOL TEACHER MAKES HER THAT WAY, MOST LIKELY-

SHE'S GRUFF AND HOMELY- BUT TRIXIE SPEAKS VERY HIGHLY OF HER-

Bum Voyage

Look Out, Annie

Going for a Ride

95

En Route

Breakers Ahead

A Leap in the Dark

Eternal Vigilance

YESSIR, SANDY— THAT WAS ABOUT TH CLOSEST CALL I EVER HAD— WE'VE GIVEN MISS TREAT TH' SLIP, BUT WE'RE NOT OUT OF DANGER YET BY A LONG SHOT— NEARLY DARK, BUT THERE'S A NICE MOON—

COME ON— WE'VE GOT TO GET A LONG WAY FROM HERE IN A HURRY— SHE'LL OFFER A REWARD FOR US, MOST LIKELY, AND IF WE'RE SEEN WE'LL BE SUNK—

BUT IF WE TRAVEL ONLY AFTER DARK WE'LL BE PRETTY SAFE— JIGGERS! HERE COMES A CAR— QUICK— INTO TH' GRASS AND LIE FLAT—

I'D 'A' SWORE I SEEN SOMETHIN' RUN ACROST TH' ROAD, JUST AS WE CAME OVER THAT HILL—

BOB·CAT, MEBBY— PLENTY OF EM AROUND HERE—

Dough, but No Bread

THERE'S A GOOD-SIZED TOWN DOWN THERE IN THE VALLEY— WE COULD GET A SWELL MEAL THERE, BUT I'M SCARED TO GO NEAR THE PLACE—

DADDY' GAVE ME A ROLL FOR SPENDIN' MONEY, JUST 'FORE HE LEFT— MISS TREAT DIDN'T KNOW ABOUT IT, THANK GOODNESS—

BUT WHAT GOOD IS MONEY IF YOU CAN'T SPEND IT? IT'S A CINCH THEY'RE LOOKIN' FOR ME IN THESE PARTS—

OOOH-- MY STUMMICK— BUT WE CAN GO WITHOUT EATIN' A LITTLE FARTHER— BEIN' HUNGRY BEATS GOIN' TO TH' REFORMATORY—

The Villain Still Pursues Her

AW, SHUX— WE MUST HAVE, COME FAR ENOUGH BY NOW— NOBODY IS LOOKIN' FOR US ANY MORE, ANYWAY— C'MON, SANDY— WE'LL FIND A RESTAURANT IN THIS TOWN AND EAT—

LEAPIN' LIZARDS! LOOK— "REWARD"— AND IT'S ALL ABOUT ME AND IT'S SIGNED BY TH' SHERIFF— THAT'S MISS TREAT'S WORK—

COME ON, SANDY— WE'RE 'GETTIN' OUT O' HERE— LUCKY WE DIDN'T GET FAR ENOUGH INTO TOWN TO BE NOTICED—

I'M SORRY, SANDY— I KNOW YOU'RE AWFUL HUNGRY— BUT WE'LL HAVE TO WAIT A LITTLE LONGER— MAYBE ONE O' THESE APPLES WOULDN'T HURT YOU—

Company for Breakfast

No-Good Money

Did I Say No?

At "High-Gate School"

The Good Ferry

River, Stay Away from My Door

Ask Me Another

No Turning Back

Cosmic City

Welcome, Stranger

The Eyes Have It

Nice People

The Willing Worker

Fate

Home, Sweet Home

Down on the Farm

Running the Gantlet

Pleased to Meet You

107

The Pariah

Misery Loves Company

Gus

A Kindly Man

A Tough Spot

O. K., Chief

110

In the Middle

A Girl of Action

Her Chief Defender

Not for Just a Day

Chief's Orders

A Heel Without a Soul

Stop Thief!

Tom Take

Disaster

A Tip from a Tom Cat

Not Mad—Only Angry

Law and Orders

What Will the Morrow Bring?

The Payoff

A Sound Investment

Good in the Worst of Us

Clip the Coupon

The Perfect Alibi

Sharing His Luck

So It's to Be War, Eh?

Slightly Used

No Sale

Roused for Action

Over the Top

Business Turns the Corner

Big Business

His Master's Voice

Opportunity Knocks

The Picket

Fighting for a Job

In These Days a Job's a Job

Reward

No Fooling

Her Hero

Her Champion

128

Never Say Die

Fire and Brimstone

Knowledge Is Power

That's the Spirit

Just a Guess

Circumstantial Evidence

Fine Words

Overheard

The Problem

Local Welfare

I TELL YOU IT'S DISGRACEFUL THAT MILLIONS OF OUR FELLOW MEN ARE DESTITUTE— MANY ARE HUNGRY— I SAY SOMETHING MUST BE DONE ABOUT IT—

SURE— THAT'S RIGHT— WHAT ARE YOU DOING ABOUT IT, MR. PINCHPENNY?

WHAT AM I DOING ABOUT IT? WHAT CAN ONE MAN DO WHEN MILLIONS ARE IN NEED? MILLIONS, I SAY—

YEAH, BUT THERE AREN'T OVER A DOZEN POOR PEOPLE REALLY IN NEED, AROUND COSMIC CITY—

AH, BUT WE SHOULD SEE THIS VITAL ISSUE AS A WHOLE— OUR FEW UNFORTUNATES ARE AS NOTHING COMPARED TO THE SUFFERING MILLIONS—

BALONEY— IF YOU REALLY WANT TO HELP, HELP THE ONES NEAR YOU— THE ONES YOU KNOW NEED HELP— LESS GENERAL BLAH AND MORE DIRECT ACTION, MOPPIN' UP YOUR SECTOR— THAT'S WHAT'LL WIN THIS WAR ON SUFFERING IN A HURRY—

11-7-32

HAROLD GRAY

Reg. U. S. Pat. Off., Copyright, 1932, by The Chicago Tribune

Get Out and Vote

✿!!! WHY, YOU MUST BE RAVIN' CRAZY TO VOTE FOR THAT FELLER— ✿✿✿✿

BAH! YOU AND YOUR CRAZY IDEAS! WHY, THAT FELLER YOU'RE VOTIN' FER ✿

11-8-32

DON'T YOU DARE TALK BACK TO ME— YOU JUST MARCH IN THERE AND VOTE— AND YOU VOTE RIGHT—

YES, DEAR—

WHEE! ANOTHER LOAD FROM WAY OUT IN THE COUNTRY, BEIN' HAULED IN TO VOTE—

VOTE

GEE, I KNOW LOTS O' FOLKS IN TH' CITY WHO NEVER VOTE, BUT ARE ALWAYS KICKIN' 'BOUT WHO IS 'LECTED— IF FOLKS EVER'WHERE WOULD GET OUT AND VOTE, I BET WE'D HAVE LOTS BETTER FOLKS 'LECTED TO OFFICE—

HAROLD GRAY

Reg. U. S. Pat. Off.; Copyright, 1932, by The Chicago Tribune.

What's This?

HM-M-M— IT MIGHT WORK, ANNIE— YOU NEVER CAN TELL—

WELL, I FIGGER IT'S WORTH TRYIN'— DON'T YOU THINK SO, MR. AGATE?

11-9-32

NOW TO LOOK AROUND FOR A GOOD SPOT— IT OUGHT TO BE RIGHT ON MAIN STREET— IT DOESN'T HAVE TO BE VERY BIG— IT'S LOCATION THAT COUNTS—

HM-M-M— NOBODY EVER USES THAT GROUND— MR. SHOPP'S STORE IS ON ONE SIDE AND MR. FORGE HAS HIS BLACKSMITH SHOP ON THE OTHER SIDE— IT'S A SWELL LOCATION—

IT'S JUST A NICE SIZE, TOO— 'BOUT EIGHT FEET WIDE AND RUNS 'WAY BACK TO THE ALLEY— YESSIR, SANDY, IT'S JUST WHAT WE WANT—

HAROLD GRAY

Reg. U. S. Pat. Off.; Copyright, 1932, by The Chicago Tribune.

The Good Earth

What a Man

Progress

136

The Center of Interest

Mum's the Word

The Indirect Approach

137

Watchful Waiting

Backed by the Press

Grand Opening

Good Business

The Menace

A Handy Memory

The Sore Head

Isn't That Just Too Bad

The Mouse Becomes a Tiger

John Hi Ho

The Subtle Celestial

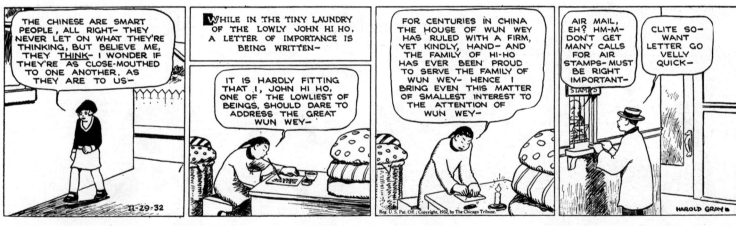

The Big Shot Goes to Work

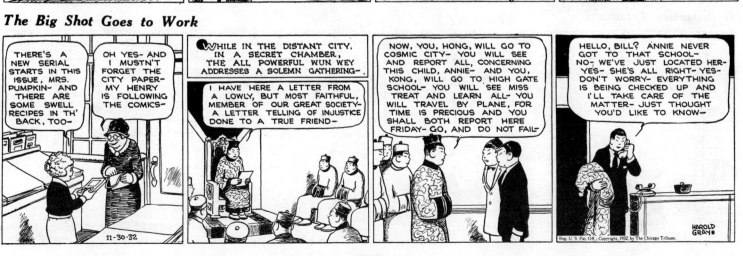

The Eyes of Wun Wey

What Will the Sentence Be?

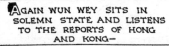

Will Justice Triumph?

145

Telepathy

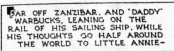

FAR OFF ZANZIBAR, AND "DADDY" WARBUCKS, LEANING ON THE RAIL OF HIS SAILING SHIP, WHILE HIS THOUGHTS GO HALF AROUND THE WORLD TO LITTLE ANNIE—

WELL, ANNIE SHOULD BE GETTING MY LETTER, ABOUT NOW, AT "HIGH GATE SCHOOL"— I'LL BET SHE'S HAVING A HIGH OLD TIME, WITH THE OTHER YOUNGSTERS THERE—

12-5-32

I WAS HALF OUT OF MY MIND, WHEN I TOLD HER GOOD-BYE— MAYBE I SHOULD HAVE BROUGHT HER ALONG— BUT NOT WITH TRIXIE— WELL, I'M FIT ONCE MORE— AND EVERYTHING IS FINE— TRIXIE, TOO, SEEMS TO HAVE CHANGED COMPLETELY—

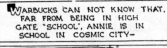

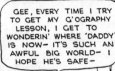

WARBUCKS CAN NOT KNOW THAT, FAR FROM BEING IN HIGH GATE "SCHOOL", ANNIE IS IN SCHOOL IN COSMIC CITY—

GEE, EVERY TIME I TRY TO GET MY G'OGRAPHY LESSON, I GET TO WONDERIN' WHERE "DADDY" IS NOW— IT'S SUCH AN AWFUL BIG WORLD— I HOPE HE'S SAFE—

HELLO, SANDY— IT WAS SWELL O' YOU TO COME TO MEET ME— SAY, SANDY— DO YOU S'POSE WE'LL EVER HEAR O' "DADDY" AGAIN? DO YUH?

ARF!

Reg. U.S. Pat. Off. Copyright, 1932, by The Chicago Tribune

The Goblins'll Get Yuh

A LETTER TO THAT RED-HEAD FROM WARBUCKS, THE OLD FOOL— OF COURSE HE THINKS THE KID'S HERE AND THAT THIS IS A SWELL GIRLS' SCHOOL— WELL, WHAT HE DOESN'T KNOW WILL NEVER HURT ANYBODY, AND IT SURE HELPS ME—

12-6-32

NO MATTER HOW BIG I MAKE THE CHECKS, THE BANK HAS HAD ITS ORDERS AND I GET TH' DOUGH— HA-HA-HA! AND IF ANYONE EVER DOES GET WISE, THEY CAN'T TOUCH ME— I'M SAFE—

E-EE!

YEOW!

Reg. U.S. Pat. Off. Copyright 1932 by The Chicago Tribune

HAROLD GRAY

Sunk Without a Trace

BUT IT'S NOT POSSIBLE—

HONEST, MR. SHERIFF— SHE WAS IN HER OFFICE, WITH TH' DOOR LOCKED— WE HEARD HER HOLLER, SORTA, AND NOW SHE'S DIS'PEARED; AND YOU SAW FOR YOURSELF TH' DOOR WAS STILL LOCKED FROM INSIDE AND ALL TH' WINDOWS SHUT—

12-7-32

MISS TREAT HAS VANISHED FROM HER OFFICE, LOCKED FROM WITHIN— NOT A TRACE, NOT A MARK OF ANY KIND, TO TELL WHAT HAPPENED— IT IS OMINOUS— SPOOKY— INCREDIBLE—

TAINT POSSIBLE—

SOMETHIN' CREEPY ABOUT ALL THIS, BOYS—

HUMPH— HERE'S A FUNNY ONE, FROM A LITTLE TOWN FIVE HUNDRED MILES FROM HERE— IT SAYS A BIG AIRPLANE, WITH NO LIGHTS, WAS SEEN TO DROP SOMETHING OUT THAT THEY THINK WAS SOMEBODY IN A PARACHUTE— IT WAS MOONLIGHT— THOUGHT THEY HEARD THIS PARTY HOLLERIN', ON TH' WAY DOWN—

AWFUL WILD COUNTRY 'ROUND THERE AND THIS 'PLANE JUST HAPPENED TO WAKE UP SOME FELLER LIVIN' IN A CABIN— HE CLAIMS TO HAVE FOUND TH' PARACHUTE AND BIG TRACKS LIGHTIN' OFF 'CROSS COUNTRY AWFUL FAST— QUEER STORY——— BUT I GOTTA KEEP MY 'TENTION ON THIS MYSTERY HERE TO HOME—

HAROLD GRAY

Reg. U.S. Pat. Off. Copyright, 1932, by The Chicago Tribune

Can Such Things Be?

Up the Hill to the Poorhouse

It's Not Right

Helping the Helpless

The Visiting Nurse

More Blessed to Give

The Face at the Window

No Doubt About It

Faith Renewed

Knit One—Pull Two

The Spirit of Christmas

Come Easy—Go Easy

Business Turns a Handspring

Christmas Eve

The Good Provider

Looking Backward

Inventory

Looking Ahead

Up the Hill and Down the Hill

12-29-32

A Mind for Business

12-30-32

Happy Days Are Here Again

12-31-32

156